Totally Bound Publishing books by January Bain

Brass Ring Sorority
Winning Casey
Chasing Lacey
Romancing Rebecca

TETRAD Group
Racing Peril
Racing the Tide
Racing the Whirlwind

Manitoba Tea & Tarot Mysteries
Magic, Mayhem & Murder
Movies, Moonlight & Magic
Moonshine, Magic & Murder

Sin City Wolf
Howl
Hunt
Honor
Hellfire

Sin City Kilts
Heart of Stone

Collections
A Little Bit Cupid: Lovestruck

Sin City Kilts

HEART OF STONE

JANUARY BAIN

Heart of Stone
ISBN # 978-1-80250-522-1
©Copyright January Bain 2023
Cover Art by Kelly Martin ©Copyright April 2023
Interior text design by Claire Siemaszkiewicz
Totally Bound Publishing

Published in 2023 by Totally Bound Publishing, United Kingdom.

Totally Bound Publishing is an imprint of Totally Entwined Group Limited.

HEART OF
STONE

Dedication

A huge thank you to my incredible editor,
Rebecca Baker, for her dedication and brilliance.
More thanks go out to all the wonderful people at
Totally Bound Publishing for making the journey
such a lovely one.
And to my darling husband, Don, thank you from
the bottom of my heart for everything.

Chapter One

Lachlan

I jumped naked from my bed, the stone floor bracing against my bare feet and the early morning chill raising quick goosebumps on my flesh. The clash of swords and shouts of men I led into battle nightly in my dreams still rang in my ears before I stretched and let the images fade away.

Last night's full moon still lingered and false dawn approached, that liminal moment when the sun has yet to appear. My ancestors believed it heralded glimpses of the future and great secrets to be shared. Me? I thought it time to be up and about.

Throwing on my shirt, kilt and boots and strapping my claymore to my back, I descended the steep steps from the north tower. Despite myself, I sensed something of import with the night's Hawthorn moon—a time of masculine power, potency and fertility, even more so than the other eleven months of the year.

Fingers of heavy mist crept across the vast estate toward me, intensifying the fresh woodsy scents of heather and moss. The low-lying fog obscured my long view of forest and hedgerows, but I knew they were there.

Untold numbers of Creigs had carved this land and battlements out of solid rock eons ago on *Eilean maddah-allaidh*, or Wolf Island as it was known to those from away, creating a legacy that would stand for generations to come. A sanctuary that was mine to oversee and care for...which included being alive to any messages sent my way.

"Okay, fine," I sighed to whomever or whatever might be listening, and, giving in, stood in the shadow of Castle Creigbourne, awaiting a glimpse of what lay beyond the ken.

An intense flickering in my peripheral vision hit my senses hard before the world disappeared entirely, sending me back to that timeless realm with no name and no season. Then a glimmering of light appeared as my third eye opened, sending flashes of blue and gold to strike my retinas. The blue of eyes and the gold of hair?

I grasped for more but the partial image vanished in an instant. "That all?" I snarked, shaking off the disquiet that the vision left in its wake. No answer came. Shrugging, I strode across the ground toward the stables. The first rays of light glinted on the dewy grass now as the sun returned, creating a field of ephemeral sparkling diamonds that never failed to put all human efforts to shame.

A series of soft chuffs broke the quiet stillness as Loki came trotting over to greet me. The legendary deerhound voted most likely to be mistaken for a large pony swiped his tail to a steady beat.

"Ah, this is the time we like best, isn't it, my Loki boy?" I bent to give his thick, wiry fur a quick rub.

He followed me into the stable, sneezing as the sharp scent of manure tickled his nose. I opened the door to Roam's stall, then led the magnificent stallion out into the alleyway and swiftly saddled him. The scent of oiled leather and clean horse flesh permeated the air, grounding me.

I swung a leg up and over the coal-black beast, both of us impatient to be off. Roam stomped the hard ground with loud thumps of his massive hooves. A destrier, he was of sturdy stock with bloodlines that harked back to tournament fields and knights in armor. He needed to be to carry the likes of this Highlander — six-foot-three of solid muscle, thanks to the daily regime of the claymore.

"Let's go."

A loud whinny of agreement followed, the stallion's breath whitening the brisk air in pillowy clouds as we surged away from Castle Creigbourne. I gave Roam his head and we raced across the glen, Loki running by our side, the three of us as ancient as any legend.

"Creigbourne Loch?" I suggested.

Roam knew the way and barely needed my touch on the reins before his strong haunches were eating up the miles across a greenscape as brilliant as any that existed on this Earth. For one brief moment I caught a glimpse of the spot where my cousin's fated mate had died. Averting my eyes, I forced the image away. It was far too beautiful a day to spend grieving for what could not be changed…although it haunted me.

The clean air and the colors of nature worked their usual wonder on me and helped to place the morning's vision in perspective. "Second sight is sometimes a gift, sometimes a curse," I told my animals. Which was the hazy impression sent to me this morning? The blue and gold could be either, depending on opinion.

Blue eyes, gold hair... Personally, I was not looking for the female prophesized by the elderly woman at last year's Spirit of Creigbourne festival. I had no need of distraction. My life in the Highlands of Scotland was filled with dealing with the needs of my clan, and I'd have it no other way. Family honor and loyalty was everything.

The edge of the loch loomed and I dismounted. My shirt tugged over my head, I threw it on the ground and took up my broadsword.

Swiping and lunging at demons and enemies, I cut a swathe across the clearing. Under the canopy of forest, I swung the claymore with precision and speed, savoring the perfectly balanced weapon in my hand. It was born of the finest steel and crafted with such remarkable precision that I'd been offered a king's ransom for its possession. *Never. Not enough money on this earth to entice me to part with the pride of clan Creig.*

An hour later, my bare chest dripping with perspiration that pooled in the ridges and valleys of my fairly earned six-pack, I removed my sturdy boots and kilt and dove into the frigid waters of Creigbourne Loch.

Sluicing back my long hair from my face, I swam out a fair distance from the rocky shore, enjoying the pull on muscles that were well-used from my workout. A bark from Loki and a whinny from Roam alerted me a second before a long-winged shadow skimmed across the water. I stilled, treading in place for a moment to observe the interloper. *Damn.*

The fierce falcon, named Tyr after a special god of bravery—a nod to my ancient Norse ancestors and to The Creig—settled on a rock nearby, his golden eyes beady and ever watchful. Then with a series of proud screeches to announce his departure, the giant bird of prey flapped his shoulders, rising into the air on powerful wings designed to catch the wind currents home or to hunt.

I swam swiftly to shore and pulled on my boots. Wrapping my kilt around my waist, uncaring of my wet skin, I whistled for Roam and Loki. "Time to head in. We have a visitor waiting," I told them.

The ride back to the castle was all too short. I curried Roam and fed him fresh carrots on top of his full share of oats and nutrients, making sure the stallion had all his needs met before heading into the conservatory where the visitor whose herald had summoned me held court.

I rolled my shoulders, the unease of dealing with whatever had prompted the visit bringing back the tension that my early morning exercise had almost eliminated. I had no choice on the matter though— when *this* visitor called, any Creig with a whit of sense answered.

I girded my loins and strode through the doorway. "Morning, Grandmother."

"Morning, Grandson," The Creig, the elder of the clan, replied, turning her stately head with its elegant upswept hairdo to present her cheek for my buss. Dressed in the customary Creigbourne tartan of black and green plaid with gold threads running through it, she perched on her throne, slight enough to be blown away in a stiff breeze. However, no one in their right mind would dare share that intel.

"Ye're soaking wet, Lachlan. Dinna ye think to bring a towel?"

I laughed. "No need. I have the constitution of an ox, the strength of a bull and the fortitude of a conqueror. Why waste time?"

"And the lasses in these parts would add…and a heart of stone," she said, then added, "Aye, but yer right, it's precious it is, time. Never enough of it."

She nodded sagely, her piercing green eyes still not requiring correction though she was ninety if she were a day. No woman admits her age, according to The Creig. She'd been thirty-nine forever before she finally quit discussing the matter entirely. Her birthday cake was only allowed one candle to this day.

"What brings you here on this fine morning?" I asked though a pall had been laid over the morning. I sat down across from her. *Might as well get it over with.* The Creig never showed up unless something difficult was afoot. Unease reared itself in my mind, making my nerves rankle. I knew the next words out of her mouth would have a cost.

"Ye're needed in America, Grandson. Cristaldo of the House of Luceres has asked for our help in a personal matter and has a business opportunity he wishes to discuss. Which means it's time to pay our debt to him."

She looked at me more keenly when I remained stubbornly silent. I detested owing a duty. So often the wishes of another burdened beyond compare.

"But I see ye already knew something of this." She pursed her lips. "If the second sight is talking to ye, then it's settled."

I ignored her last words, instead pushing myself out of the chair and beginning to pace. I preferred to think on my feet. "I have a great deal on my plate at the moment, taking care of our vast holdings. I can't just rush off to America at the whim of another."

I was venting, knowing I would have to answer the call. As head of the clan, paying the ancient debt the Creigs owed to the house of Luceres fell to me, and I would honor that, not even think about sending my brothers, Calan or Logan, or even one of our cousins.

"I knew it would come to this one day, but not now," I muttered. A warrior chooses his own path, his own battles. Of course, once I wanted something, I would not be deterred from obtaining it by any means necessary. How else could I have doubled our billions in the past decade alone? "But, of course, honor above all."

"Aye." The Creig picked up her dram of spirits she'd poured earlier. She swallowed it a single gulp. "Spectacular year."

"It is." I waited for her to come to the point.

"Was your vision any clearer this morn?" Her question hung in the air between us, those few words filled with more portent than the most dramatic soliloquy and, knowing what she was asking, I shook my head, a bit more riled than I let on.

She leaned forward to add weight to her words. "Well, ye must think of the future, Grandson. Ye are heir to all we possess, as is the right of the first born. And ye are not getting any younger." She pointed her glass at me. "And neither am I. Would you deny me grandchildren?"

I snorted. "You're going to live forever. And it's blatantly unfair, the structure of inheritance. Archaic laws that need changing."

"Be that as it may, if ye canna find your mate on this side of the water, she may exist in the new world."

Her words clanged like warning bells, especially when allied to the reason for her visit. "Grandmother, I'm not looking to upend my life. A lass from another country with a different culture causes too many complications. I have too many responsibilities right here. Obligations that cannot be set aside on the whim of another."

"We must learn from the past, but embrace the present, Grandson. You won't be the first to cross the water for your mate. Your *one*. Besides, it might lighten ye up!"

I grimaced and let The Creig's words sink in as she poured us both a drink of Scotland's finest. My life was so regimented, the needs of others firmly set before my own, as it should be for the alpha of a clan, especially one who needed to lighten Grandmother's load as she aged.

And yes, over the quickly passing years, I had become less light-hearted and more solemn, though the love of wit and laughter called strongly at times. Things an adult must set aside. *Isn't that the proper way of it? Not kicking over the traces?*

I glanced at my favorite painting of all time, hanging in its place on the conservatory wall. Backlit spectacularly by the artist, it depicted my great-grandfather doing a sleight-of-hand magic trick, a gaggle of his grandchildren huddled at his feet, their tiny faces alight with amazement.

I'd always been fascinated by stories of him, and his personality, leading to my lifelong enjoyment and practice of the art of magic, everything from close-up to illusionist tricks. My brothers had called me cracked for spending long hours at this, but I enjoyed it and had got pretty skilled.

Then, as if Great-Grandfather were calling to me, a thought struck me. If I had to visit Las Vegas, or Sin City as it was more rightly called, maybe I could recapture something of my lighter side, and do something I'd always wanted to do? Take some recompense for the interruption to my life? Could I? I looked at Great-Grandfather. *Yes.*

"Fine. But I get to do it my way," I said, crossing my arms over my chest.

The Creig's eyes gleamed with interest and she stared at me, but I remained stubbornly silent. *Where do you think I got my need to turn the world my way?* She tilted her head, as if listening to something I couldn't hear, then nodded. "Good. It's settled then. Now, how about some breakfast?"

Taken aback, I muttered, "Of course," and mulled over the situation while we ate the tempting dishes the servants brought at her request. I quickly consumed vast quantities of steak and bacon, sausage and eggs with sides of toast and oatcakes in short order. I had a great deal of preparing to do and little time to accomplish it.

"If you'll excuse me, I have somewhere I need to be."

The Creig nodded as I took my leave, her expression expressing pleasure at the outcome of our meeting. As if it were ever in doubt. I always uphold the honor of our family.

"Off with ye, grandson. I look forward to my invite."

The Creig had passed the second sight on to me, the first born, though her advancing years had added immeasurably to her ability. She knew far more than she would ever admit about what awaited me in Vegas, but it would be no use asking her to divulge it, and I was too proud to beg.

Exiting the castle, I tore off my kilt and boots, ready for my real exercise—my wolf run. Creigs were weres, our secret ancestral heritage, and this would be my last chance before heading off to Sin City. I wanted it to count. I wanted to feel the wind in my fur, the scent of life in my lungs and the world dropping away as I raced across the moors.

I pushed my way from our realm through the glimmering portal into the next dimension so tantalizingly close to ours, the process necessary to shift my energy from man to wolf, the actual transformation occurring in an instant. All those painful experiences expressed in novels? Patently untrue for any werewolf I knew — a small mercy.

The world had now mutated to an array of colors unknown to the human eye, blacks and browns and grays with subtle shadings that my brain converted to what my human side saw — blues and greens, yellow and reds. I breathed in deeply, my olfactory nerves sharpened by the cool, moist morning Highland air, each scent more rousing than the last.

A chorus of howls erupted in the distance, begging me to join them. I took off at a quick lope, overcome with a sense of urgency. This might be my last chance for a while.

I slipped off the bonds of duty, my worries over the Creig estate and concerns about the journey to America. Instead, I embraced my animal nature, letting it take over. The grasses compressed beneath my massive paws, acting like a springboard to my prowling.

I stood taller and larger than the thought-to-be-extinct dire wolf and, blessed with sharper tracking ability, soon picked up the scent trail of Calan and Logan.

Around a thick stand of birch and oak trees, I caught sight of them with my superior vision, my younger brothers lying in ambush, hoping to catch me unaware. My wolf mouth stretched in a grin.

I'd teach them a thing or two.

Chapter Two

Esme

"My late husband always said he would come back for me...send me a message if he was okay. I've been waiting and waiting, hoping against hope this is the night I get a message." I dabbed a tissue to my eyes.

The grandmotherly woman that had taken an interest in my plight moved in closer and patted my back, sharing the moment with me as we stood amid the small group of people milling around the entrance to the Vegas theater, waiting for the popular psychic of the day who was scheduled to appear.

"Cheer up, dear. I've got a good feeling that tonight will be your turn to hear from beyond the veil."

"Thank you. I pray you're right. He's been gone almost a year now, struck down by a drunk driver not far from this spot. I'm hoping with the theater this close to where it happened, that it might help?" I shredded the tissue with my fingers and turned away from the press of people.

"It surely can't hurt. Spirits tend to linger where they were torn from this life." The kindly woman with the faded blue eyes and bouffant white hair leaned in. "I, too, lost a husband. But I was much older than you when it happened. How old are you, twenty-seven or so? You must have gotten married so young."

"I'm twenty-three." A streak of vanity made me ask myself why everyone thought I was older than I am. "But yes, I was only eighteen when we got married. We were high school sweethearts, married only a year when he was taken. I know it's a cliché, but he was my whole world. I was putting him through college by dealing on the Strip."

"That was so good of you. What was he studying to be?"

"A doctor…a pediatrician. He wanted to help sick children." Finished blowing my nose, I bit my bottom lip, trying to gather myself, and cast a glance over the couple of people nearest to us—a couple of middle-aged women and a lone guy on his phone.

"Aw, that's such a loss for the world, dear. No wonder you feel so distraught. Have you had any help since the accident? Gotten some therapy for your grieving? I know when my Norm passed, I found sitting at his graveside and talking about my day was therapeutic. And for once, he couldn't interrupt."

A twinkle sparked in the old woman's eyes. "I'm sorry if that was disrespectful in any way. I just wanted to make you feel a bit better. I've always found a bit of humor helpful. My momma always said life is too serious to be taken too seriously."

"No, that's fine." I hiccuped, trying to hold back my emotions. "It's nice to have someone to talk to."

The doors to the theater sprang open at that moment and people began to file in, the guy who'd been playing on his phone one of the first to move. *Eager.*

"Are you okay to go in?" the elderly woman asked, checking the doorway and looking anxious to head inside.

"Yes, I want to see if I can learn something, anything at all really, about Mathew."

"Nice name, dear. I'm Anna Nicole Smith by the way. Isn't that a hoot!" The woman laughed outright this time, her eyes crinkling at the edges. It took me a second to realize who she was referring to, a centerfold from the nineties. We hurried in. "And what are you called?"

"Esme Luceres." I groaned, not meaning to spill my last name and not in public like this but caught up for a moment in Anna's merriment.

Luceres. I didn't bother to mention I was the poor relation, though the name Luceres carried more baggage and expectations than most, my relatives being billionaires and all. *Doesn't get much worse than the too rich, arrogant, shifting alpha bastards who think they know all about how I should live my life. Oh, and I'm one of the rare ones not capable of shifting into a furry wolf, like that's the be-all and end-all.*

Except, my dreams of chasing across the desert with a mate, experiencing the wind in my fur, did kind of bug me. Something I wouldn't be sharing with the House of Luceres any time soon. Of course, the Luceres name still opened doors, but I tried very hard not to capitalize on that, wanting to lead my life on my own terms.

"Pretty name for a pretty girl. I remember when I had smooth skin and masses of blonde hair like you. Heaven knows, doesn't seem all that long ago. But that's interesting, now that I look closer, *you* remind me a whole lot of that pinup gal. You should consider flaunting those considerable assets, dear, before it all heads south. That's my take on life."

"Ah, thanks for the advice, Anna." I choked out my reply. She patted my arm again then tottered off to join the other audience members walking through the arched doorway.

Inside, half-amused and half-mortified, I held out my ticket to the usher. Okay, I did conceal my curves under clothing that hid more than it flaunted. Being taken seriously by others was important to me. I didn't ever want to be mistaken for a bimbo.

My business depended on my attaining work from people interested in finding out why their dwelling went bump in the night, so there was no need for me to show up looking fancy. *Imagine humping all the equipment needed in a pencil skirt, anyway!*

I found I was seated not far from the lovely Anna and when I glanced over, she blessed me with a reassuring smile.

The lights flashed on stage, the music cued and out walked the man of the hour. Winston McIvor, psychic medium, available to channel the spirits for those in need. *Oh, really?* I peered hard…yes, he looked a little familiar…

The man certainly had loads of charisma, oozing confidence and intrigue with ease, though all I cared about was what he had to say. He strutted right up to the edge of the stage, his high and tight Elvis-esque hairstyle seeming to vibrate with energy while his eyes brimmed with keen interest.

We had more than enough impersonators on the Strip to ensure the King would never die. But this one had the kind of male posture that screamed *I'll take care of it all if you'll just allow me to assist you, little lady.*

I held my breath, waiting for him to speak, keeping my eyes on the prize. I—like most everyone in the room, I betted—had filled out a slip of paper with a name and question. Had mine been drawn this time? I'd been stalking the man for a week, hoping to be picked. I glanced at my phone—I had only an hour before I needed to get to my moonlighting job at the House of Shadows Museum where I managed groups for our famous flashlight tour. The rather fun night job kept me in funds to help prop up my fledging business of Ghoststompers, Inc.

Winston now put a theatrical hand to his high forehead, his eyes closed. I didn't care what he did as long as he got to the part that mattered to me. "Is there a young lady here in great need of contacting her husband who passed away over a year ago? He wanted to be a doctor?"

I sat up straighter but didn't put up my hand yet. I just waited, needing to hear what would come next.

"The young man has a message for his wife, Esme."

I liked my name. It meant esteemed and loved. My mother had always made sure I felt loved growing up, even when she was widowed and lost all her money. I'm one of those rare poor Luceres relatives, can't shift and definitely don't want much to do with them.

"Your husband is saying that it's time, that you need to get over your grief, that it's holding you back from moving on."

My pulse jacked up, the hair on the back of my neck tingled.

"I'm getting more now…" Winston slanted his head to the right, like he was listening to someone. "Yes, your husband wants you to know that he's happy where he is and that he wants you to open your heart to finding love again."

Anger, something always a bit too close to the surface, began to roil inside me.

"Is Esme here? Young, beautiful girl in her twenties, according to her husband."

I felt Anna's eyes on me. I couldn't look at her, knowing I would give myself away. This was definitely the guy who'd been standing close to us outside the theater, texting on his phone, a baseball cap pulled down over his forehead. He'd gleaned any information he had from knowing my name, which I shouldn't have shared with the elderly woman outside the theater, had probably done a quick internet search on me and now thought to pull me in and use it to his advantage.

"One last message for Esme that maybe someone can pass along. Your mother is also doing fine. She's with her family up in heaven—"

That's it! You read that my mother recently passed, and now you're moving into exploitative territory, buddy!

I jumped to my feet, unable to contain my emotions. "Fat lot you know! I've never been married—I laid a trap for you! You're a *fraud*, Mr. Winston. A man who takes advantage of others' grief and pain, and I'm going to report you to the Nevada state ethics board."

Someone grabbed my arm from behind. Damn, a security guard. He loomed over me and pointed one hand close to my nose, so close I was tempted to bite the offending finger. "You! Out! Before we call the cops."

Every eye in the house staring at me, I swallowed my chagrin, my cheeks burning bright red. "Fine, I'm leaving anyway! Who needs this? The man's a fake...a charlatan. Get a life, people, and stay away from creeps like that! They're just looking to steal your money," I blustered. I really didn't want to be arrested again, just draw attention to the obvious — that so-called psychics were almost always fake.

"Miss?" The angry usher with the grim expression escorted me unceremoniously to the door.

"No need to call the cops. I'm leaving now." I had made my point, hoping I'd changed at least one mind tonight. My mom had used up every spare dime on looking for answers from mediums. This was my way to save others, and their families, the grief. Sure, it bore risks, but what right-minded endeavor didn't?

"Just don't come back here. Got it? Next time you won't get off so lightly."

I nodded, not trusting myself to speak. *Push it any further and I would find my ass in the slammer. Again.*

Outside in the twilight of the evening, I stood in front of the theater and took a few deep breaths to regain control. *Ten. Nine. Eight...* As I stood there, my line of sight moved upward to a newly installed billboard promotional across the road, so new the workmen were just now taking down their scaffolding and loading their gear on a flatbed truck.

Wow.

Just...wow.

I swallowed, hard, my mouth going dry from the larger-than-life image of a Highland Scotsman in nothing but a kilt just about bursting out of the billboard's one-hundred-foot-high frame, ready to sack cities and plunder women. His long golden-brown locks flowed back in the breeze and his square-jawed face screamed *I know what I want and how to get it.* Who on earth was this uber-warrior?

I was too focused to see anything else and stumbled backward, right into a huge body. I would have fallen, but two strong arms held me upright. The scent of Irish

Spring soap and heather tantalized my nostrils. Twisting around in his arms, I found my breasts pushed against a broad chest.

"I'm okay. You can let me go now," I protested. Crap, why were my nipples pebbling? I shivered, excitement racing through me.

He did let me go then and I was able to see my rescuer. Well, soon as I looked *way* up. Oh, my goddess! The stunning Scotsman from the billboard! His chest wasn't bare now, but, oh my, he wore a kilt well. With more flair than most celebrities do dressed in Armani or Prada strutting the red carpet.

"Are you okay, lass?" he asked in a low, throaty voice that shattered my last nerve, his piercing green eyes totally focused on mine. The greenest pair of eyes I'd ever seen in my life. *Mesmerizing.* Then realization took hold as I breathed in more of his amazing scent. *Ah, I know where all that animal magnetism and confidence is stemming from — he's one of us.* Not a wolf from America with that accent, of course, but from Scotland. *That* explained his I-can-have-anything-I-want confidence.

I straightened my dress, looking away from his intense eyes to notice my nipples were still poking through the material. *Please, don't look there.* But his gaze, with no other obvious place to land, flicked down my body. The crazy thing was, standing too close to a complete stranger, I could swear my body recognized him on some elementary level. It was disconcerting and baffling.

But his calm, aloof demeanor coupled with a certain light in his eyes was too much.

"I'm fine. Excuse me, I have to go." It was then I noticed the group of females hovering nearby and what appeared to be his entourage of roadies and assorted characters...maybe groupies? It looked like I might have just fallen into an autograph session. "Seems you're rather busy as it is."

"I didn't catch your name?" He moved a step closer and I had to work extra hard not to step back or throw myself forward into his arms. *What the hell is going on? Only the biggest case of lust-at-first-sight in the history of the world.* And no way would I *ever* breathe a word of that to a single soul as long as I lived.

"That's because I didn't throw it." I crossed my arms over my breasts in an effort to conceal them. But of course, that just pushed them higher, threatening to spill out of the top of my dress. Okay, I did look a little too much like Anna Nicole Smith for comfort.

"Oh, *Lach...lan!*" A coy voice rang out. "I need you over here for a moment. Pretty please!"

To his credit, the tall drink of intoxicating vitamin water didn't look thrilled about the interruption. Though it was rather hard to tell, just a slight tightness of his jaw and a certain glint in his eye giving it away — an enigmatic, stoic Scotsman, no doubt. What would it take to make him break through that gruff barrier?

"You'd better go. We don't want a riot on our hands."

"Why did the usher escort you out of the theater just now with a warning not to come back?" he asked bluntly, making me startle. *What business was it of his?*

"It was nothing."

His commanding look suggested he didn't believe me, which upped my annoyance factor. I stared him down, neither of us willing to give an inch. When he moved a step closer, I panicked. My mind scrambled for an excuse, any excuse.

"I was just playing a part, okay? Practicing my sleuthing skills for an upcoming Netflix production of...yes...*Exposure*. A new series about debunking charlatans and frauds in the psychic industry. We need crowdsourcing. You interested?" *If you're going to tell a fib, make it a whopper.* This part was going to be such fun to share with my friend and business partner Meghan.

"*Exposure*. I might be able to open my wallet for such a venture. That's if you give both sides fair play. Some mediums are real, especially those with second sight. How much do you need, *m'eudail*?" An almost imperceptible twinkle in his arresting emerald eyes made my heart flutter anew.

Oh my, he's a Big. Bad. Wolf. Imagine calling me his darling on first meeting.

I held up a hand, letting him know I was waving off his offer. "Nothing yet. Early stages, you understand. But we'll soon have a presence on social media. But I need to run. Got an important report to write for the director and producer." I began backing away from distraction, gritting my teeth. My ovaries high-fiving each other wasn't helping.

"Here, take these."

I automatically took what he pulled from his...sporran? Whatever it was called, it was housed far too close to his cock. *Why am I thinking about his cock, for heaven's sake!*

I grabbed the small slips of stock paper and marched away, far too aware of his possible view of my ass bouncing up and down from the excessive movement. I could feel the intensity of his stare from the fifty-yard line. It made me look back for a sec, catching him watching me. I swallowed hard and glanced away from his steady, brooding look, certain I had just experienced an out-of-body moment.

It was then I realized what I was holding. Two expensive almost-sitting-on-the-stage tickets and a backstage pass to the Hypnotic Highland Warrior show. Yeah, right. Like I'd go to see him in person. *No one can hypnotize me.* I was about to throw the tickets in the nearest trash barrel when I reconsidered. *Wait.* How much more fun would this be if I could get the goods on him?

Because this kilt-wearing, intense-eyed, muscles-for-days Scotsman needed taking down a peg or ten...and I was the gal to do it.

Chapter Three

Lachlan

I strode into the Glitter Palace Casino, taking in the opulent surroundings of marble and high ceilings decorated with an artist's expert rendition of cherubs cavorting. Lavish fountains supposedly added a soothing touch to the senses while throngs of people busy looking to lose their money to the house milled around the gambling tables and slot machines. Vastly different from the quiet pastoral regions of *Eilean maddah-allaidh.*

Alistair, my faithful manservant, followed me inside, carting an armload of gifts for Cristaldo. Respect for a fellow alpha meant acknowledging our past connections and celebrating our future dealings, something I would never stint on. Family honor was everything and especially to the proud Creigs. But what boon or favor left over from ancient days did the House of Luceres' alpha need? My curiosity heightened as the elevator ascended to Cristaldo's penthouse.

"After you, sire," Alistair said. We both knew we were most likely on camera and had planned accordingly. He knocked briskly, then moved back from the custom-carved double-doors. A realistic rendition of wolves on the hunt carved into the thick wood and burnished in dark stain commanded the view from floor to ceiling. I approved of this far more than the cherubs downstairs.

The heavy doors flew open and there stood Cristaldo in a black suit, white shirt and black tie, framed by a spectacular view of the Vegas Strip skyline.

"Welcome, Lachlan Creig of the Highland Heathens Clan," he announced, his powerful wolf-like presence obvious even to the naked eye. I stood a few inches taller than the Luceres alpha, a satisfying reality. We shook hands, testing the strength of our grips. I had not seen Cristaldo in over a decade, my own clan concerns chewing up all my time. The space in the interval had been good to the man. He stood confident and comfortable in his own skin.

"I come bearing gifts."

"It is an honor to have you here," he responded with a nod.

Alistair handed over the first box, filled with the finest spring water. I waited for the alpha's reaction and was not disappointed.

"Water?" Cristaldo's eyebrows rose as he took in the label on the box. "How thoughtful to come all this way with bottled water."

I hid my smile. "And when you're thirsty for something more palatable, we've brought you something of far more renown from the Scottish Highlands. Our finest single malt whiskey, Macallan Lalique. I trust you will find it comparable to your regular drink."

"Yes, I'm quite certain it will be as smooth as the Dalmore 62. I insist we send you home a crate of our finest for your private stock." Cristaldo answered in kind, playing the game well.

I nodded my acceptance of the lavish gift. Alistair took his leave, flashing me a meaningful glance of approval on his way by.

"Well, now that we've got the niceties out of the way, shall we sit and discuss why I called you here?"

We sat across from one another on matching throne-like chairs with high backs and thick cushions. The Luceres did know how to live.

"I apologize. We would have invited you to share your illusionist act here with us, but we have a situation where it's best if a certain person is not aware of our alliance. It's a sensitive family matter. Would you care for a drink?"

"I would."

Sipping the excellent single malt with appreciation, I gave a look around at the magnificent surroundings. "You did okay for yourself." A vast understatement, but my host took it in stride.

"Yes, both our extended families have done well over the centuries. We share a certain history, you and I, between your clansmen and our house."

"Yes...and one that will never be forgotten. The Creigs are in your debt for all that was done to assist in saving targeted females during the burning times. That is a debt that can never be repaid in full." It was a time no one liked to think about or speak of, but it needed to be mentioned as part of formal proceedings.

Cristaldo acknowledged my words with a solemn nod. "Our move to New York City during that hellish period allowed us even more opportunities to hide those suspected of witchcraft." He shook his head in dismay, the expression in his eyes grim. "A terrible tragedy and a dark time in history. Impossible to believe that it happened in today's world."

"It still happens occasionally in remote parts of the world to this day," I said with a grimace. "Barbaric."

"And when the House of Luceres has called upon your community over the centuries, the call has always been answered by the alpha. We are in debt to you as well for that assistance." Cristaldo spoke with pride, though his eyes were shadowed by the past.

We drank in silence for a moment, steeped in endless memories of another time and place.

Finally, Cristaldo stirred himself and set his empty glass down, leaning forward in his chair. "The reason for my call is two-fold. Shall we discuss business first?"

I nodded, preferring to stay away from the personal issue as long as possible.

"As you know, crypto-currency has become big business this century. Unfortunately, a lot of start-ups have scammed the populace, not backing up their claims and vanishing with all the profits."

"Despicable companies, lacking in honor," I acknowledged.

"I want us to combine forces and start a brand-new online banking system." He went on, filling me in on the myriad details. I suggested some ideas to his new structure and within the hour we had a deal. Business was the easy part. I was worried far more about the second part. I girded my loins when Cristaldo switched gears and I sensed something of what was coming.

"The personal part is a bit more sensitive. A young cousin, raised under difficult circumstances, lost first her father, who had an irrational dislike of our family connections, then her mother...lost her money on false prophets. The girl is troubled and living a precarious existence on the periphery of our family—it seems no matter how we try to bring Esme closer, she pulls away and chooses a path that can lead to either exposing our existence or causing her own downfall."

The name caught me—caught and stopped me. "Esme Luceres? I met the lass last night in front of the theater where Winston McIvor was performing." The image of the beauty flooded my mind. I had researched her right after meeting her, using facial recognition techniques after finding her on CCTV footage located on the street corner nearby. I'd never had such a strong reaction to a woman before—her intoxicating scent still lingered. And now this. There are no coincidences in the mystical realm, and this one reeked of intent. *The blue of eyes and the gold of hair?* "The lass so filled with the need to expose fraud among psychics she nearly got herself arrested."

Cristaldo grimaced again. "Exactly. She's in over her head and needs a fresh perspective. One I believe a staunch Highlander with family and honor as his main focus can provide. One of my people, a witch and an empath, even senses and predicts trouble for the girl, and since she won't accept Luceres' help, just keep her safe. That's all I ask."

I nodded acknowledgment, owning my truth. "And you want me to keep her in the dark about this request." Yes, that explained why the invite to play at the Glitter Palace had not been offered as would have been expected.

"I would appreciate it a great deal that it be kept a secret from everyone, not just Esme. Our family prefers handling all matters quietly, which is why I called upon you, Lachlan. I knew you'd understand with your background. The House of Luceres will owe you a great boon in the future for helping us with this. You have my word."

I gave my solemn approval and acceptance. "It would be my great pleasure to help you with Esme."

Cristaldo refilled our glasses with the nectar of the gods. "To the honor, health and well-being of our mutual families," he toasted, knocking the rim of my glass to seal the deal.

I took a sip of the whiskey. "Very smooth. Comparable to our own private label."

My mind raced with the implications of my new responsibility of looking out for Esme. Surely it would be easy to show her the error of her ways? Look who she was up against—Lachlan, alpha of the Highland Heathens Clan, a true force of nature with generations of staunch kinsmen at his back.

Yes, this would be simple enough...

Chapter Four

Esme

Twenty-four hours later and I was sitting—correction—make that *fuming* in the audience of the casino that was featuring the Highlander who I could not get out of my brain.

"The MCM Grandstand Ballroom welcomes the biggest, baddest illusionist and mind-defying hypnotist in recent memory to its main stage! Ladies and gentlemen, please give a ringing round of applause for Lachlan Creig and his Hypnotic Highland Warrior show!"

The fog machine and the live orchestra cued, and in mere seconds a huge otherworldly giant of a man stepped through the rising mist to the resounding beat of an ancient drum. His bared chest, all golden ropes of muscles, gleamed in the sudden firelight that danced shadows on the walls of curtains and pillars, making some of the women around me gasp in surprise.

I just stared with a skeptical eye, pressing my thighs tighter together. Just because he'd given me about the best seat in the house didn't mean I wouldn't hold him accountable for any shenanigans he might try to pull tonight.

But, to give him his due, he was a magnificent sight. He must work out in the gym. A *lot*. His muscles looked crafted of pure marble. His hair was flowing backward from his ridiculously handsome face thanks to a wind machine that was earning its keep. I was absolutely dead certain that all the females in the audience could only hope a stiff breeze pushed aside that glamorous kilt for a check of the goods beneath. Some even had fingers twitching in their laps like they'd like to do the deed themselves.

Actually, looking around, I saw most of the audience were women. *Figures.* He probably handed out tickets to every woman he met just to get a bevy of beauties to choose from after the show.

"I am Lachlan Creig of the Highland Heathens Clan, *gie it laldy*, meaning to give it my best, here in Las Vegas, Nevada, with a house full of wonder to mesmerize and astound you! And without further ado, let the show begin!"

The warmth of his demeanor, so much less aloof than our meeting, the outstanding charisma of his delivery and his rumbling bass tone with the smooth and sexy Scottish accent had the audience in the palm of his hands in a nanosecond. Me, I hardly noticed, being so busy watching for plot holes. Just how fake was this guy? No one looked like *that* and was also gifted. No way, no how.

The showman strutted across the stage, the light bouncing off him as he opened the door of a huge cage that had thick steel bars…and demonstrated that it was empty and strong by striking it with a hammer. The high-pitched ringing sound resounded inside the theater, making it obvious the cage was the real deal. It was also suspended above the floor with no place to hide anything, instantly making me suspicious.

"How strong are these bars?" he asks the audience with a smirk. "Shall we see!"

He stepped inside and closed the gate, locking himself in with a giant padlock. Instantly a drape descended for maybe one full second. Ha, he was going to cheat! My bet was on him turning into a wolf. Bloody hell, he'd be in trouble for doing that! I sat up straighter, waiting with bated breath.

Instead, what had that mountain of a man done when the curtain lifted? He'd vanished. Gone, leaving the entire audience gasping. How was it possible? There was nowhere to go and I could see right into the cage from my vantage point. Mystified, I shook my head in disbelief. The curtain dropped again and when it was raised, there he was. Every shining inch of him.

He then did something I'd never seen before. He began to bend the bars apart, his muscles straining, nearly popping out of his fine tan flesh. Oh my, so strong it made people around me gasp with shock. The bars squeaked and grated loudly in protest, but the man persisted. When it was wide enough, he stepped through the opening and leaped to the floor.

The audience burst into huge applause, cheering and whistling. I hadn't even recovered from the shock of watching all that pumping man flesh exhibiting the kind of strength that makes a woman's knees weak when he changed direction. *This guy really could bear a person away to the ends of the earth if he wanted to.*

"I've been entranced by the magic of snow falling at midnight on the moors of the Highlands since I was a lad learning magic at the knee of my great-grandfather." The stage lighting changed, revealing a starry Van Gogh sky with swirling stars and a pregnant moonscape. The mystical backdrop set off a sense of otherworldliness to his skin, anointing it with a bluish glow. The moment of ancient timelessness caused the audience to fall into rapt silence, their faces keen with interest.

"Let winter come." He lifted his hands to the sky, standing in front of the mystical moon backdrop, as if praying. From his palms, crystals of pure white snow began to flow upward then slowly drift down to the stage, turning into a shower of golden stars around his feet. But instead of stopping in a couple of seconds like I'd seen other illusionists' work do, it continued to flow from his hands until the air began to almost vibrate with an infinity of snowflakes glowing like diamonds in the haze of the bluish light. It collected around his feet until a flurry of glittery stars anointed the stage.

Ohs and ahs escaped the audience's rounded mouths as the man directed the weather. *How in the hell is he doing that?* Before I could figure it out, he started a new trick.

"For my next act I need a volunteer." He prowled to the side of the stage and looked down at the row I was sitting in, right up front and center. *Don't. You. Dare.*

"Would the bonny lass with the lovely blonde hair and wee frown in the enchanting red dress please join me up on stage?" He gave a wicked smile that demonstrated his excellent dentistry and held out one huge hand with the super-bulging biceps toward me, beckoning me with his mesmerizing green eyes. I hesitated. "Or are you afraid of being hypnotized, *thasgaidh?*"

Hell no. Game on. And touché for the use of another Gaelic endearment term.

I smiled sweetly and rose, taking his hand. He swept me onto the stage in one graceful movement, my feet leaving the ground, his touch coursing through me like an electrical current.

"A chair for the lovely Esme Luceres," he called out. An assistant scurried to do his bidding, bringing one forward.

"How did you know my name?" I asked with a scowl, tugging my hand free of his.

"Magic, Esme. Magic is in the air tonight. Trust me, and the world will offer up its riches."

I snorted. "Yeah, right."

Not to be dissuaded, he gestured at the chair and I plunked myself down. This could prove interesting. Like anyone could hypnotize me. Spookier entities than Lachlan had tried and failed in my Ghoststompers, Inc. business. *All duly recorded for posterity.*

"This is a special pendulum made from the golden mask of a long dead deity that was purported to live in Atlantis, the fabled isle, before it sank into the sea never to be seen again. It has hidden powers that open a channel into the brain, promising enlightenment and ancient wisdom." He held the large golden disk up for the audience to observe, the odd marks that were engraved into the surface looking like rune symbols. "Do you like to dance?"

Ah-ha. "No." I shook my head so hard I nearly gave myself a concussion. "I never dance, no time for it. And I've got two left feet," I admitted.

"Keep your eye on the coin as it flows back and forth, Esme. See the past...let it come forward and bring forth its power. Back and forth, back and forth. Relax, relax..."

I duly tracked the gleaming coin with my eyes, finding it rather soothing. Something to focus on while this charlatan played his silly game.

"That's right. *Back and forth...*"

Lachlan

Ah, the lovely Esme Luceres who doesn't believe in the power of suggestion. Another hypnotist would not choose her, but see who else in the audience was more amenable. But she was a far more worthy challenge.

"Back and forth...sleepy now, so relaxed your limbs are heavy. Look deep into my eyes, see the beginning of time, when the world began glooming from the mists." This was the most important part of it. She had to shift her focus to me.

It took a few hushed seconds, but then those fascinating sapphire-colored eyes of hers were staring deep into mine. *Liquid pools of infinity.* Her light floral perfume tickled my nose, and the beginnings of arousal lingered in the air, lighting a path straight to my cock. My wolf pushed against me, wanting out, nearly unseating me for a split-second of torment. We'd been for a run in the desert earlier to work off my frustrations at not bedding the lass, or anyone for that matter, since we'd met on the Strip. Now I had to force him back into submission, and with the world watching.

"You want something very badly, bonnie Esme...to dance the tango, the dance of passion. See yourself with clicking heels and clapping hands, enticing me to enter the arena inhabited only by lovers. Stand now and take my hand. Let me pull you tight to the circle of life."

Her eyes widened farther, and her head went up proudly, her back straight as an arrow. I helped her to her feet, whirling her into the dance of lust. It didn't matter if she knew the steps — I'd make this non-dancer look good.

And I did, our feet pounding the stage in rhythm, the audience egging us on, cheering, having heard that the woman could not dance. But tonight, Esme shone, a vision of beauty and longing as she exhibited the steps to perfection. When her foot rose to land on my shoulder, letting her dress flow away from her thighs, I nearly lost it, the delicious fragrance emitted from her pussy sending signals racing straight to my willing cock. I spun her away to gather myself, wanting nothing more than to take her right there and then. To sink into all that womanly flesh and sail us to the end of the world and back. *Die the little death.*

When the music ended, I bent her over at the waist and bestowed a kiss on her…a kiss I never wanted to end. Her soft lips locked onto mine, her tongue twirling against my own, enticing me in further. Her breath entered my body, the sweet taste of her essence bringing a rush of sensation unlike any other.

The focus became all her as she locked her arms around my neck giving me all the license I needed to allow my mouth to seek answers as I crushed her to me, feeling her heart beat in tandem with my own. The kiss would not have ended if not for the stage lights flashing around us and the orchestra hitting a sour note. I let her go then and handed her a rose with a flourish, but held on to her as we bowed for the audience though in truth she was holding on just as tightly to me. But this woman was not getting away without my finding answers to that powerful pull.

Then she shook her head, waking from the trance. She gave me a horrified look, her jaw dropping open. "What did you do to me?" she shouted.

"Nothing—mesmerism can't *make* anyone do anything they don't want to do. Otherwise, there'd be chickens and murderers galore running around doing someone's dirty deeds," I said, perhaps a bit too smug for having made her dance amazingly well with two left feet. I was, after all, still in the sway of the sensation of holding her sweet body in my arms and sharing that amazing kiss.

"No way! You're not getting away with it! You cheated! You...you...big lug!" She swung at me then, taking me completely by surprise.

The slap didn't hurt, of course, but I sensed my security detail about to descend on us and that I could not have. I needed to shut this down. Now. To protect Esme above all.

"You're a fake! This is all a con. You're, you're a w —" She finally stopped herself, realizing that she could not say what she wanted to say. It was forbidden, a line that once crossed, could not be uncrossed. Then the ire of many powerful families would descend on her pretty blonde head.

"I used my gifts born of ancient bloodlines and hundreds of hours honing my mind, body and spirit, Esme. There's no crime in that," I said, standing firm, trying to make her see reason. I had earned all that I had become and I would not apologize for that.

The security guards rushed on stage. I commanded them to stay back with an outstretched hand raised high in their direction. The team halted their approach instantly.

"The police have been called, Mr. Lachlan. You want me to take her to our security holding center until they get here?" one of the burly guards asked, looking a little too pleased with the idea in my opinion. *No one touches Esme. No one but me.*

"No need, I've had my say. I'll leave," she said.

"Afraid we can't let you do that. You attacked the star of the show for no reason," the guard said with a pointed glance. "We all saw it. We have it on camera."

She blushed, her hands clenching at her sides. But to her credit she stopped herself from doing anything else to embarrass herself.

Esme couldn't hurt me physically if she tried all day long. I admired that she was a strong, opinionated woman who would be an equal partner in any situation. A woman who would keep a man in line, something even an alpha needs on occasion. At least according to The Creig, anyway.

"No need for that," I said. "She was under the sway of my hypnotic suggestions." I gave the lass a pointed look, just throwing it out there. All my life I'd wanted a woman to give it back to me. "Or maybe it was her sway I was under?"

"I'm not the one that tries to sway *anyone*. We all have free will to choose," she huffed.

"Is that so?" At least I had her full attention now. "So, you're saying that you *chose* to dance with me, kiss me," I teased. "That you can dance and that hypnotism had nothing to do with it? You can't have it both ways, Miss Luceres."

"I'll have it any way I want! As to who hypnotized who, I guess we'll never know for certain. Maybe someone slipped ecstasy into my drink? Or maybe I had dental surgery and I'm still under the influence of laughing gas? That's more likely than you being in control of my body," she said with a smirk, thinking she'd outwitted me. Though I did note she held on to the rose I had given her before exiting the stage, taking my keen interest with her.

Chapter Five

Esme

I was fit to be tied. An uneasy sleep last night after the altercation at the Hypnotic Highland Warrior show had put me in a right jangly kind of mood where all I could think about was that darn man. *Hypnotism, my ass. Then he thinks to blame me for it all!*

Okay, we had danced exceedingly well together. I touched my lips with the impossible-to-get-rid-of memory of his kissing me. The feel of his warm mouth pressed to mine, his minty breath, that massive chest. And such strong arms on that man, like tree trunks, and everything seeming fueled by such irrepressible passion. It was like touching electricity, the way it coursed through my body as we danced. *Damn, there I go again!*

Honk!

Making myself pay better attention to the road and its other users, I parked my Ghoststompers, Inc. van in the staff section of the lot then entered the House of Shadows Museum through the side door, my face aflame with indignation.

At least my enjoyment for the upcoming stroke-of-midnight flashlight tour increased as I changed into my period costume, an elaborate, 1900s-inspired, stiff black dress that gave the impression I was a gothic Edwardian-era housekeeper. Cosplay was such a lark! And the paying visitors seemed to enjoy it. My only complaint was that the bonnet made peripheral vision difficult, though the shadows it added to my face compensated, adding a general spookiness to my spiel for the tour.

The best part of this ghostly package, the most expensive tour by far that we offered, was the small number of the participants and the fact they would be given a free run of the place for a period of time at the end of the tour. That was always such creepy fun.

A final check in the mirror that my bonnet was tied on properly and I hurried through the dimly lit museum with all the macabre displays to open the front door where I liked to greet my guests. I stepped out onto the wide veranda, noting the eight people lined up waiting to enter, their faces ghostly under the streetlamps that were also period pieces. The black wrought-iron structures were right out of Jack the Ripper, Whitechapel stories. I shuddered. Thoughts of Jack always brought a shiver of fear down my spine.

I counted heads. There were nine names on the clipboard list—maybe someone had chickened out? One man carried an EMF reader that lit up when ghosts are located and a digital tape recorder with an external microphone and that was fine. We even allowed modern ghost boxes. I did notice he knew enough to wear an old-fashioned wind-up watch to avoid a dead battery. As long as they didn't take photos and signed the waiver agreement that stated the museum wouldn't be held responsible for anyone dying of fright on the premises, they could check for ghosts all they wanted.

I struck a pose, hands raised to the night sky, and spoke the usual words of greeting. "Welcome, brave guests, to the infamous House of Shadows. I trust that nothing untoward will befall you here."

A giggle or two followed my pronouncement. One elderly lady clapped her hands.

"Tonight, prepare yourselves to hear the tales of the macabre, the stuff of nightmares. You will see displays set in the very rooms where the original crimes occurred, and maybe be visited by someone from beyond the ken. If anyone chooses to leave, now is your final chance to depart unscathed."

The eight participants looked sideways at one another, but everyone stood their ground. I took a moment to assess them. Two elderly ladies, arm in arm, one touristy twentysomething male, a May-December romance between a balding middle-aged man who kept grinning at the young woman fawning all over him, the tall ghost investigator, one taller, thinner man who appeared to be channeling a character from *Faust*, and one heavyset man in a fedora that covered his eyes. Hmm, Mr. December looked somewhat familiar. Where had I seen him before? The memory eluded me.

The most striking of the group of course was the guy going for the Mephistophelian effect. The thirtyish man had dyed jet-black hair and eyebrows, and was dressed all in black. *Way past gothic to truly odd. Maybe an actor?* No way those evil slanted eyebrows were natural, though the pall of depression hanging around him had a ring of legitimacy to it.

"Anyone here suffer from seizures? A heart condition requiring medication? Do you all have your printed waivers with you? If not, you will be asked to sign another one."

A flurry of paper was handed over and I smoothed them out to check that each was properly signed. I was in too much of a hurry to do more than give a cursory look, but the number of sheets added up, which was all that mattered. One per customer.

Just then a sleek black limo entered the parking lot at a fair clip and I looked up to observe the driver jumping out and opening the back door. I inwardly groaned. The ninth person was a possible celebrity. They were always the most annoying and demanding. And more often than not late. A huge mountain of a man climbed out along with a giant animal that I presumed was a dog.

I recognized him immediately. *No. Frigging. Way.* The very man haunting me. I rolled my eyes to the heavens. So, this was payback for some indiscretion, right? I promised not to piss anyone off more than necessary tonight and maybe someone could think about lifting this curse?

Suck it up, Esme. You have a job to do. Patently ignoring the man with the dog by his side, who strode confidently toward us like he did on stage as if the *entire* female population of the world was ready to drop their panties at his feet, I opened the creaky door, preparing to usher my tour group inside.

"Welcome, dear guests, to the House of Shadows," I announced. Now if only I could slam the door before *he* made it through! Because, damn it, I did not have a change of underwear in my locker.

"Excuse me, *mo chridhe*, but have we met before?" he asked, looming over me with his oh-so-charming smile. He moved quickly for a big man. And for heaven's sake, who called someone *my heart* if they'd only met once?

"I think I'd remember that," I shot back. "Meeting you. Who's your pal?"

"Hmm, nice to be thought of as memorable," he said, smooth as silk. "And this is Loki, my deerhound. Say hi, boy."

The humongous dog gave me an inquiring look, his head cocked to one side as if deciding if I was friend or foe.

"Hi Loki, I'm Esme. Nice to meet you."

He slipped his head under my hand, demanding attention. *Huh, just like his owner.*

"Hmm, he doesn't take to everyone so quickly. Normally he's quite standoffish. A person has to prove they're trustworthy first." Lachlan gave an approving nod.

"I think it demonstrates his good taste," I teased. I bent down and gave the dog a good scratching behind the ears. "Right, boy?"

"Is it okay if he comes inside? If not, my driver can take him for a walk."

I pursed my lips. "The owner never said we specifically *can't* have a dog inside. I have no problem with it. But I'll need to check with the others, just in case someone has a concern about dogs...you know... allergies, or scared of them or something? Let me check for you."

But before I could, Loki's fur stood on end and he dashed for the door, barking as if the gates of hell had just opened up.

"Stand down, Loki!" Lachlan demanded. The dog immediately stopped moving, sitting at attention. He kept his eyes focused on the open doorway though, as if he expected trouble at any second.

"I guess that settles that. Something inside has him spooked. Most likely a ghost. Loki's not too fond of them. Come on, boy." The big man, the dog at his side, strode back to the limo. The image kind of tugged at my heart. I'd have liked to get to know Loki better. Too bad his master was *him*.

Lachlan

I led Loki across the parking lot to the limo. His reaction to Esme was heartwarming. And surprising. I meant it when I said it took him time to warm up to another person. But why was the beautiful lass wearing such a terrible getup? She looked like a spinster, a woman incapable of enjoying the sensual pursuits that made life worth the living. I had the sudden urge to buy her dresses, fancy little numbers that highlighted her considerable assets. Easy-to-remove dresses that swirled and swayed with every moment, catching the sunlight. Or firelight. The stiff black monstrosity she was wearing now should be taken out to the backyard and burned to cinders.

I secured Loki with John, one of my limo drivers, and rejoined the small gathering, just in time for Esme to lead us to the first exhibit. She talked on the way, her face half-hidden by the bonnet, caressed by shadow. I listened, intrigued by her keen interest and professionalism for the job.

"Please don't touch anything, no matter how tempting, or I will have to report you to the principal and he might demand detention. No one wants that!"

Hmm, this wolf wouldn't mind. Visions of being in detention together with her danced in my head. Perhaps with her wearing a short plaid skirt with no panties, bent over the teacher's desk?

She continued, "You're welcome to take all the photos you'd like of the *outside* of the House of Shadows, but, please, none inside. And if one shows up with a ghostly image, the owners would appreciate it if you'd email them to the web address on the back of your tickets."

"Do I need to turn over my record of the night's events?" a man who was clearly a ghost hunter asked with a frown. "Nothing was said about that and I don't think that would be right at all."

"No, what you record is all yours to keep," Esme soothed the annoyed man before I had the opportunity for a word with him about his reckless rudeness. "Now, let me introduce you to our first murder scene. We'll head to the attic and work our way back down to the main floor. That way when you get tired, you're close to home base."

I moved to join her now that her opening remarks were concluded, leaning down and whispering in her ear. Her lovely scent filled me, making me aroused and soothed both at the same time. "I wouldn't mind at all being kept in detention, for as long as you like, Miss Luceres."

"You wouldn't like it nearly as much as you think," she quipped back. "I'm an expert at making grown men weep for their mothers. And I've always been told, the bigger they are, the harder they fall."

"I've always heard it told as the bigger they are, the *bigger* they are. If you get my drift."

She worked hard to suppress a smile, though a small hiccup escaped. "Oh, I get your drift just fine, Mr. Creig."

"It's Lachlan, or Laird if you prefer."

"I had another idea. How about I call you — "

"Are we going to continue this tour?" Ghost hunter man interrupted our exchange, earning a steely frown from me. He turned pale, but he did shut up.

Esme led us up the wide old-fashioned staircase with the prerequisite dark-stained ornate banister, then up a narrow set of stairs to the third floor. Then one more flight of even narrower steps to the attic. She went to open the door at the top of the final set of stairs, but as hard as she tried to pull it open, it held fast. I was about to move around her and assist when she turned around and gave a professional smile.

"Sorry, folks, someone must have locked it after the last tour. It normally opens easily. I'll be back in a jiff."

She kept a smile on her face as she squeezed past all of us lined up on the staircase, barely making it by me with my extra-wide shoulders. But as soon as she was gone, the door swung open on its own accord. *Hmm. Part of the show?* We ended up ushering ourselves inside a room with low ceilings and faded wallpaper of what might have been old country roses. By the ominous emotions still lingering and haunting the space, thrumming with an uneasiness that verged on hysteria, it was obvious tragedies had occurred here, and often.

A few of the people were huffing and puffing by the time we entered the attic. Not Esme, when she came flying into the room two minutes later. She was in prime shape. I'd appreciated watching that gorgeous backside of hers lead the way earlier and wished there were more stairs to climb. I also couldn't get her all to myself soon enough.

I took a cursory visual of the dimly lit attic. Stains ran down the low walls like rusty tears while antique lanterns covered in cobwebs could barely penetrate the gloom, leaving the corners in complete darkness. Two rows of single beds set against the outer walls were roped off. The musty air made one elderly woman sneeze and her companion handed her a tissue.

The depressing atmosphere of the room made the man with the electronic devices perk up, walking about officiously with the equipment over his shoulder and the microphone held out before him. Would he find any residue energy on his fancy machine? I never needed such things, having found out early on that I was a lightning rod for spirits still lingering in our world. Most just needed a little nudge to move on. Belief in haunts is fairly common in my country and we have our own rituals to deal with them.

"Seems the ghosts decided to let us in after all!" Esme smiled and picked up the thread again. "House of Shadows was originally named Fearon House, after the family that owned it. It was built in nineteen hundred and six, not long after Vegas was founded. This is the infamous Blood Room. The housemaids kept in this room were slowly drained of the precious substance at night, one by one, down in the basement, an area we will visit later. The lady of the manor bathed in their blood, thinking it kept her young."

"Like Elizabeth Bathory?" One of the elderly pair spoke up, her beady eyes bright and birdlike.

"A very similar case, in fact," Esme agreed with a shudder. "It concerned the Hungarian Countess, Erma Taigi, who bought the house in nineteen hundred and nine after the Fearon family fled. A terrible tragedy had befallen the first family to live on these premises. The father had been called out by a cuckolded husband. Apparently, the man had been a notorious philanderer." Esme grimaced. "He was killed by a bullet to the heart in a duel at dawn, leaving the family heavily in debt."

"Did it work, do you know, dear? Using the blood to remain young?" the woman pressed, her companion looking a bit embarrassed at the question.

"That I don't know, but I do know she only recruited virgins. Their blood was highly valued and she paid their families well when they later died from 'consumption', probably to help suppress rumors." Esme made air quotes around the word.

"What happened next has been set down in the annals of history. The countess herself was hung in the basement by parties unknown, her body slashed with a thousand cuts and left to bleed out. She is still regularly sighted at the windows of this house, though only one picture exists of her wearing the distinctive high, crownlike headgear that distinguished her from others."

"Gory details indeed! Our very own Hungarian countess in Vegas. Imagine that, sister, finding eternal youth?" the elderly woman said in awe. "And now we'll never know if it worked because she was murdered. Shame. I'd give my right arm for a youth potion. And all my jewels to have one night with *him*." She nodded her head to the left, indicating me.

I smiled at the woman. *Harmless flirting.* "Never needed any jewels to be enticed to spend time with a lady," I said with aplomb. "And you don't need any youth serum. Every tiny imperfection when the product of a life well lived, is a blessing, my grandmother was fond of saying."

Of course I exaggerated. The Creig had fought the good fight against admitting any such thing soon as she quit celebrating birthdays years ago. My words drew an intriguing look of surprise from Esme though.

The woman tittered happily and whispered something into her companion's ear, and both sisters now eyed me with interest.

The only other couple in our group, a middle-aged man with a younger woman huddled to him, seemed to be taking far more interest in each other than the tour. None of us could move far apart, with areas being roped off to keep the participants from venturing further into the room. The pair were whispering, though with my acute hearing, I caught every word. Hmm, seemed she wanted to know if he had told someone about them yet. *Aww, the wife.* So, it was like that. When he admitted the truth, she pulled away angrily. I predicted no bedroom fun tonight for him, and I didn't need any special powers of mindreading for that one.

The ghost man didn't seem nearly as impressed, his machine remaining quiet, his expression dismayed. "Well, this is a rip-off. Nada. Nothing at all in this room."

I gave him a look and he backed up a step.

"Perhaps we frightened her off?" Esme said with a small smile playing about those full pink lips. The kiss we'd shared last night came back in all its wild passion-fuelled glory. I wanted to press myself against her and kiss her silly until she surrendered to me again. Just not here, in these creepy surroundings — though thankfully the ghosts seemed calm enough tonight — but back in my huge suite that overlooked the city. I wanted us surrounded by starlight and the fragrance of fresh flowers for our first time together.

What would be her bloom of choice? I figured her for a lover of gardenias with her jasmine-scented perfume. I'd fill the bedroom with vases of the blooms. My blood heated with the image of her lying among the blossoms, her skin pink and rosy from the bath, all dewy fresh —

"Any more questions before we move on? Mr. Lachlan? Anything to share? Anything at all?" She quirked an exquisite eyebrow at me, her mouth pursed.

I set my legs farther apart under my kilt, my partially buttoned white dress shirt no hindrance to getting her full attention. The electricity between us was off the charts. Yes, there was something I wanted to share with her. My cock. It hadn't let up its magnetic pull of true north toward her since she'd fallen into my arms in front of the billboard. It was as if my body recognized hers. A mystery still to be plundered.

"Perhaps a magic trick or two?" I stepped forward, a sense that there was just the two of us in the world, that no one else mattered a whit, and pulled a jasmine-scented gardenia from behind her ear and tucked it into her bonnet. The scent lingered between us and I had the urge to sweep her into my arms, bear her down the stairs and squire her to my hotel. I might have done it too, if a voice hadn't intruded on my thoughts.

"Say, I know you. You're that illusionist headlining on the Vegas Strip! You were attacked on stage last night by a woman who didn't like being hypnotized and made to dance. Ha, turned out she could! She looked kind of like our guide here." The twenty-something tourist finally had words to offer.

"I have no idea what you're talking about. If you'll follow me, we'll get on with the tour." Obviously stung by the comment, Esme whirled about and led the Lightning Brigade charge down all three flights of stairs to the main exhibits floor. I dashed down the steps right behind her, the rest of the group forgotten in my pursuit.

"Are you missing anything?" I whispered in her ear when I caught up to her.

"What do you mean?" she asked, her eyes narrowing with suspicion.

"An event on one of the other floors? Surely something of interest must have happened on one of them? Something to share with us? With me?" I touched her arm, feeling the answering shimmer inside her, echoing my own. The connection between us was undeniable. Off-the-charts intense. What would it be like to be truly together? Locked in each other's arms...

Her pupils dilated and her cheeks grew rosy, all signs of arousal. "Why are you doing this to me? Why are you here?" She trembled, making my heart squeeze.

"Just taking the tour, same as any other person. And I'm doing nothing to you that you don't feel as well." I ran my fingers down her arm, the fabric no hindrance to the power of the acute sensation, seconds away from kissing her again. Claiming her. It was as if another force of nature had taken over entirely. *The blue of eyes and the gold of hair?*

"Yes, you are. You're using some kind of mind control to make me feel this way." She clearly wanted to move away, but she stood still, looking into my eyes. "Who are you really, Lachlan Creig?"

"Help! Help!"

An eardrum-destroying scream bounced off the walls, demanding our attention.

Everyone froze while I raced back up the stairs in the direction of the din. Rounding the corner into the attic room at full tilt, I discovered the young female on the dusty floor, holding the older man's bald head on her lap, rocking back and forth.

"What is it, lass?" I bent down to check out the man and found no obvious signs of injury. I laid two fingers against the man's neck to check for a pulse. *Nothing.*

"I think it's his heart," the young girl wailed. "One minute he was fine, then he dropped to the floor like a rock, clutching his chest. We were all milling about, trying to be the first out the door to follow the guide, and he just collapsed. Oh, God, is he going to be okay? Say something, Danny, please!" Tears ran down her face, bringing black streaks of makeup with them.

"We have an emergency at the House of Shadows Museum. Please, hurry! A man is suspected of having a heart attack. Unconscious. We're in the attic, top floor. Yes, Esme Luceres, an employee." Esme spoke into her cell phone, her expression tightened by concern. She had followed me up the stairs and now crouched on her knees beside me. Shaken as she had to be from our interaction, I had to admire her quick response to a dire situation. When she gave me a questioning look, I shook my head.

"Does he have a pulse?"

"No. I'm going to start CPR. Can you help me lay him out straight?"

Esme laid her hand on the young woman's shoulder who hovered in the way. "We need to move him."

The girl nodded and let me in closer to deal with him. I began CPR, knowing it was futile, but not willing to give up hope. For anyone else, it would be exhausting work, but I kept at it for the full ten minutes before we heard sirens, then footsteps on the stairs.

By then the spirit had spoken and I knew some of the truth. I chastised myself for not having paid closer attention earlier — perhaps I could have prevented the tragedy, but Esme had taken front and center in my mind. She was now not only Loki-approved, a new standard for me, but watching her work, helping during the crisis, all had taken my respect for her up a notch. She was the kind of person worthy of getting to know better. And I had Cristaldo's blessing to do so.

The paramedics swarmed in and took over. I glanced around the attic, spotting something that shouldn't be there...

Chapter Six

Esme

"What an awful thing." I shook my head as I joined my tour on the main floor, not really speaking to anyone in particular, just trying to get my mind around what had occurred. "Another death in the museum, and it happens in the attic of all places."

"Do you think maybe the energy from the lingering ghosts had anything to do with it?" the ghost investigator asked with a bit too ghoulish an interest for my roiling stomach.

We had been all told to wait in the foyer to answer their questions before leaving, so we were stuck here. I could feel Lachlan's interest, sensing his presence even when I turned away. Annoyed didn't cover it. One of the elderly sisters was at the moment being interviewed, first up to bat.

"I think this has a real-world explanation," I said crisply. "The man had a known heart condition."

"And he wasn't doing it any favors spending time with such a young, energetic woman," the other sister said, sharing a knowing look around.

"It was more than his heart," Lachlan said, his expression thoughtful. "Something powerful interrupted the man's electrical system."

"You can't know that," I said, aghast at the idea. I narrowed my eyes at Lachlan before checking out the response of the others in our group. The twenty-something looked pale, like he'd seen a ghost. The heavyset man in the fedora stood off to one side, drinking from a water bottle. Mephistophelian man looked grimmer still, constantly adjusting his mustache. Was one of them a murderer? Was that what Lachlan was suggesting?

"Could be a spirit, just like I said," the ghost investigator crowed.

I shared a glance with Lachlan. What had he picked up on? I had to know. Closing the distance between us, I got right to it, pointing my finger at him accusingly. Every minute since this man had entered my life had been a complete disruption of the norm. One minute flirting, the next wanting to throw daggers. And the worst part was, I didn't know how much more of my hormones running amok I could take without going ballistic or throwing myself at him. "What did you see? You got to the room first."

"I didn't see any more than you did, Esme."

"Then why suggest such a thing?" There was something he wasn't telling me. I was certain of it. A murder on my watch wouldn't look good, not good at all. Of course, there was a dead man to think about. If he had been killed, he deserved to have his day of justice.

"The coroner will investigate every possibility. And, as it happened, I noticed a syringe lying on the floor nearby. It's evidence, so I didn't touch it. It may have been filled with a substance used to induce a massive heart attack. Such things are possible, and with everyone in such close proximity, milling about the attic and being stuck on the stairs, any one of us could have injected the man."

"A syringe has no business being there. I don't like the sound of this." I chewed on my bottom lip, thinking about it. Lachlan sounded so certain, his demeanor calm and confident. There was more to this than just a syringe found on the floor.

"It will have to be investigated. I'm just telling you to be prepared in case it's ruled a murder."

"*Murdered.*" The elderly woman's eyes lit up, round as dinnerplates. "The curse is real then. I've read about it. Sinners will be held accountable by the ghosts of Fearon House, mark my word. That man is likely married to someone else and only spending time with the young lady. *Tsk-tsk.*"

I knew all about the curse, of course, but today I had been so disturbed to have Lachlan joining us I had committed an oversight of not mentioning it. Or getting to the litany of secret passageways. Or the two rooms that dead-ended, built for who knows what reason. Where was my head at? But I had been interrupted, consoling myself that I would have rallied. Darn it, but I needed to regain some control of this situation.

"If that were the case, a lot more people would have died in this house than have. He can't be the first sinner to come walking through those doors in decades. There hasn't been a murder here since the nineteen fifties when the mob owned this house for three decades," I countered.

"Yes, and who knows how many spirits of gangsters still reside in the basement. That's where they killed them, you know, dear, down there." The woman pointed at the floorboards, nearly salivating with the telling. I got her then. She was either a tour guide wannabee or an amateur sleuth. Not uncommon. Like a student in a classroom, they wanted the attention of everyone in the room. Well, that explained all that shameless flirting with *him*.

"Will we get the chance to check out the basement? It was listed on the tour site," the ghost investigator asked, his lips pursed.

"I don't think so. Not this time."

A series of groans followed my words.

"But I'm certain I can offer you all rain checks or your money back, whichever you prefer."

"I'm definitely coming back here." The older woman nodded with enthusiasm though her sister looked doubtful.

"Me too," ghost guy added.

"I'll take my money back," goth guy said.

The guy in the fedora just ignored us all, texting on his phone with a nonchalance I envied. A man might have just been murdered in our midst, all of us possible suspects, but missing a text was the most important thing to worry about?

I spent the next few minutes sorting out the ticket situation to everyone's satisfaction.

"Lachlan Creig?" a voice boomed out. One of the detectives had stepped back into the room and gave a searching glance around.

Lachlan strode away, his kilt swaying from the speed of his confident actions, and vanished from view. The man was just too much. Energy and charisma to burn. My insides were still quaking from our earlier encounter, demanding answers.

But I didn't go to bed with everyone I was attracted to...well, not that I was usually this turned on by a man. *Okay, make that never.* But he'd made his interest in me abundantly clear. Pulling a flower from behind my ear—could he be more obvious? Dancing the tango. *Phttt.* Didn't make up for tricking me on stage and somehow hypnotizing me. How the hell had he done that?

Now he was here when a possible murder happened? The guy brought too much energy to the universe and the whirlwind that surrounded him. I needed a breather. How long was all this going to take? And more importantly, what would the owners of the museum think if it turned out a murder had happened here? Darn it, they might have to close down for a while, meaning I would be out of a job, a job I badly needed.

I needed to solve this thing, all by myself if necessary.

While the others drifted away to perch on various seats around the foyer, I opened a search on my phone, a sudden interest to learn all about poisons that mimic a heart attack. I was halfway to keying in the words when I stopped, realizing what a fool I'd be. Sure, offer a breadcrumb trail to the police. It might be after the fact, but it wouldn't look good. I quickly deleted the search words.

Now what? I drilled my fingernails on the reception desk, thinking.

Then the detective was back and calling my name. Nervous, I wiped my damp hands on my skirt and, bracing my shoulders, hurried after the man.

I was surprised to find Lachlan still in the room, standing with arms folded over his chest, sucking up all the oxygen as per usual. Even the two detectives looked off at having the not-so-friendly-looking giant there with them. I was about to protest, but he shook his head at me, a clear warning in his eyes. What was he up to? I was about to call him out when the detective spoke up.

"Let me introduce myself. I'm Detective Tom Olson and this is my partner, Detective Sean Jackson."

"Nice to meet you both," I said, bracing myself. No matter that I knew I was innocent, something about being hauled before two detectives was a little unsettling. I'd bet that was true for anyone unless they were used to it and knew how to work the system.

Maybe I should have been a lawyer? No, I would be bored to tears. So much more fun sleuthing out and debunking the paranormal. But I had a bigger problem...did they know about my past arrest? Because in light of this new situation, my actions looked a bit rash.

"Esme Luceres, you're employed to be a guide for the museum. Correct?" Detective Olson asked, his eyes dead serious as they bored into mine. He was middle-aged and a bit overweight. His sports jacket, though off the rack, fit him well enough.

"Yes, that's right."

The other detective, younger than the first, was hunched over and making notes on the meeting on a white pad of paper.

"Luceres," he said thoughtfully. "Are you related to the owners of the Glitter Palace?"

I inwardly groaned. *Here it comes.* "Yes."

"What is a Luceres doing giving tours in a museum? Your family is as rich as Midas according to the papers and their bank accounts."

"Not all of us are willing to live our life to suit or serve others. I'm determined to make my own way in this world and stay far, far away from the uber-rich."

"Perhaps not, though service to others is a fine pursuit, in my opinion," Lachlan said.

"Serving others is not the same as being asked to work in a casino or give up on your dreams of running your own business," I spat.

What I hoped no one knew or brought up was the stain on my family. The string of men who took advantage of my mom when my dad passed. Her using up all available money to pay their outrageous fees to let my mother feel she was contacting him from beyond the grave. She would never believe me when I said he had passed on. That there was no way to be in touch because the conmen had kept her dream alive as long as she had a dollar left to spend.

A scandal made even deeper by the fact that my father, though I had loved him dearly, had failings of his own. A man who had lived his life in contempt of being a Luceres, keeping our family away from the mainstream, swearing about how bad they were for us. How they looked down on us, the poor relations. My adding to the scandal with some of my earlier actions probably would be best forgotten as well. Still, I wished it could have been different. I longed for more family. *Well, suck it up, Esme, it is what it is.*

"As I recall there's a little more to *that* story than you not wanting to work in a casino," the detective said dryly with an arch of his eyebrows. "There was that altercation in the Waldorf when you interrupted a private séance of some pretty important people who took offense to your revelations. I believe you were arrested?"

A rush of indignation added physical discomfort to my growing annoyance. "That man was nothing but a fraud, taking advantage of people who believed his con. A showman with no substance."

"Be that as it may, you did pay a fine and were given a warning."

I gave a stiff nod of my head, wishing that I had maybe handled it a bit better, not drawn such attention to myself. *Sometimes I fly off the handle too easily.* But I wanted to warn people that they were being taken advantage of. Was that so wrong? Sure, there was a price to be paid, and to date I had been willing to pay it. But now, looking back, I realized I could have made better decisions, drawn less attention to myself.

"Now, can you walk us through tonight's events, beginning when you arrived for work."

And so I did, in exacting detail, all that had happened, though it didn't seem like much. But enough that it kept Detective Sean Jackson busy scrambling to get it all down. Why didn't they use a voice recorder? It would be easier. Maybe the detective was old-school. He certainly seemed it, not wasting time on pleasantries. But did he have to bring up old wounds? Probably to undermine an interviewee's self confidence, make them feel lesser than. Well, I was having nothing of what he was shoveling.

"And did you see the syringe lying on the floor?" Another very piercing glance at me.

I shook my head, sensing the tension in the room at the question. "No, I did not. I was too busy explaining the history of the place then helping Lachlan aid the poor man." I swallowed hard at the memory of the man on the floor. "I only heard about it when Lachlan mentioned it."

"Aw, your lawyer." The man's eyebrows rose with some skepticism.

So that was how you pulled it off. Though I had to admit, it was a relief to have some support in the room. Like I'd admit to that anytime soon.

"Did you know the deceased, Danny McCoy?"

"McCoy?" Oh shit, the name was all too familiar.

My expression must have given me away because the detective's look became even more sharp-edged.

"You knew the man?"

"I didn't realize who he was until now. A former customer who solicited the services of my business." I chewed on a thumbnail, remembering back. *Nothing good to report here.* Why did he have to be the one? The bastard that wouldn't pay Ghoststompers, Inc. after we revealed that no ghost walked the halls of his hotel, that it was 'haunted' by old pipes and plumbing issues.

"What business is that, Miss Luceres?"

"I head up Ghoststompers, Inc. We either catch ghosts or debunk paranormal explanations for hauntings and such." I was proud of having started my own business and was working very hard to turn it into a viable enterprise.

"And Danny McCoy used these services of late?"

"Yes," I answered cautiously. "I was invited to stay at his hotel to find out the name and history of the ghost the proprietors were certain stalked the residence."

"And did you find one?"

I shook my head. "No, there was no ghost. Just bad plumbing. Most so-called hauntings are revealed to have other causes."

"I take it the owners were happy about this, not being haunted?"

"Actually, no. I think they were hoping for a ghost. Good for business. They had plans to advertise it on the popular haunted hotel website for tourists."

"That's very interesting, Miss Luceres."

"Will there be anything else, Detective?" I asked, desperate to get the hell out of there before they discovered that the McCoys hadn't paid me, pissed that no ghost had walked the halls of their hotel. I had done my job, just not to their satisfaction. The invoice was still outstanding on my company's books.

"Not for now. But I need your contact numbers in case we have further questions."

I gave the information to Detective Olson and scrambled to my feet, eager to get away. Of course, Lachlan was hard on my heels as I escaped the room. I pulled him into the staff office before turning on him, closing the door to make damn sure we were out of earshot of the others. I had just two little words to say to him.

"You're fired!"

Chapter Seven

Lachlan

"You need my help more than you think," I said to the stormy-faced Esme. "This is a murder investigation we're right smack-dab in the middle of here. There's no time for dissention between us." Surely the lass accepted she needed my help with none of her Luceres male pack members here to protect her? I would step into their place and take care of her for as long as required, whether she liked it or not. Any male shifter would do the same.

Esme gave me a calculating look, her head tilted sideways. "What do you know of it? You're hiding something from me, I'm more and more certain of it. So spill." She crossed her arms over those lovely breasts, tapping one dainty foot on the floor.

"I have the second sight and understand more than most. And anyone present in that room could have injected the man with the chemical compound in that syringe. We're all suspects at the moment."

"You, a seer? I don't think so. It's all part of your act, right?"

I shook my head, tamping down my annoyance. "You will discover I'm a man of my word. What I say I am, I am." She didn't need to know that Cristaldo and I were on the same page about her needing to be carefully watched over, that she could be her own worst enemy. I was honor bound not to let her in on things.

"Prove it then. Who killed the man in the attic, if indeed he was murdered? Who injected him?" She pounced on me like a cat dangling after a bit of string. But such a pretty cat. Though I would have to watch out for those sharp claws digging into anything other than my bare back.

But she had me there. The ghost of Danny McCoy hadn't named his murderer, just moaned the accusation from the other side. The urgent sense was growing by the minute that I had better dig a whole lot further into this case. Esme was involved up to her eyeballs, whether she realized it or not. The connection to her having caried out a ghost investigation at his place of business spelled trouble. She needed my help more than she knew. Thank goodness Cristaldo had had the good sense to call upon me.

"Danny didn't share the name of the killer. He might not have known, just put two and two together when he lay dying. They will find a small needle mark on his right arm, between his elbow and his shoulder. Mark my words."

"Sounds like you know too much about it. Did the police think maybe *you* had something to do with it and you're just covering your tracks, Mr. Lachlan Creig?"

"I didn't share my second sight with the cops."

"Well, if they do discover you know about the entry point of the needle in question, I guarantee they will be interested. But it won't come from me. I don't point fingers, unlike others."

Stalemate. Or...was it? A sudden idea occurred to me, one I liked even better as I shared it. "I think we should investigate this together. With my gifts and your...shall I say skepticism...we can solve this in no time. We'd make a great team."

And what a perfect way to spend more time with her without having to conjure up excuses, because I wasn't letting Esme out of my sight.

"No, not going to happen, no way." She might as well have swirled a red cape at a bull. Her reluctance was my command.

"What? You afraid of a little competition, lass? Worried I can best you at the game?" I quirked my lips into a smile, wanting to see her response to my throwing down the gauntlet.

"I can best you at *any* game! I'm very talented at finding out things. If you hadn't shown up here needing my attention, I'd have noticed what was going on. Plus, I'm open to experiencing ghosts as well if one exists, and nothing appeared to me. You might just be making this all up."

"They're not so uncommon. You might be missing some. Then how about a little wager? The one who discovers the name of the murderer wins the day."

She pursed her lips, a flash of interest shining in those deep blue eyes. "Any stakes I choose?"

"You choose yours and I choose mine." I knew exactly what I wanted of her.

"What are yours?" she asked.

"You have to be my assistant for a day. Do everything I ask for twenty-four hours, *everything*." I smirked, imagining her in the costume of my choice helping me on stage. A little red number, short skirt with high heels. *Every man's go-to fantasy.* And maybe just to add a dash of flair to the outfit, a gold ribbon tied in a bow set around that graceful neck.

"And if I win, you have to do the same. Work with me in my business, helping out here at the museum and doing *everything* I say. And no insisting on any physical interaction allowed. We understand each other?" She narrowed her eyes at me for emphasis, tapping that dainty foot extra hard.

"If you say so?" I shrugged. Time spent together would prove the futility of that stance. This was the most fun I'd had with a female in so long—I couldn't remember the last time. While her beauty was arresting, her spirit and personality drew me in far more. And she was Loki-approved, which said a lot.

"Okay, we need to make a plan of action." She chewed on a fingernail, contemplating things. "I think the girlfriend and wife needs to be checked out. He was here with a younger woman, not really trying to hide it, so maybe it's a simple case of jealousy?"

"Jealousy's a prime motive. And the girlfriend was having words with the victim over telling the wife about her and asking for a divorce. So is inheriting money, and a hotel and all the trappings are a big draw. Was the victim successful?"

"Well, he didn't pay me, but the hotel's worth quite a bit. Good location and a lot of tourist traffic."

"Wait. He didn't pay you, Esme?" That was bad news on every front. As soon as the detectives knew that, they'd be all over her. A disgruntled business owner would have a prime motive. Of course, a case could be made that she wouldn't do such a thing on her home turf where she'd most likely be suspected.

"Someone may be setting you up," I said.

She bit her bottom lip, her eyes widened by worry. "If only I hadn't drawn attention to myself going after others in the past. I mean, they know I've been arrested. This is bad. My connections to all this…"

"Don't you worry. We'll solve this in no time and point the finger at the real murderer. You have my word on it." *An alpha always protects his woman.* That was the moment I realized just how interested I was in Miss Esme Luceres. I'd only known her for two days and I wanted to be her champion. Her white knight in shining armor. *The blue of eyes and the gold of hair?*

"You mean, I'll solve it," she said, rallying.

Aw, there was the spunk I admired.

"So, the plan is we check out all the other people on the tour, book into his former hotel and check on the wife's situation. I'll make arrangements right now." I pulled out my phone. "What's the name of the hotel?'

"The Hatfield & McCoy," she said with a straight face.

Even I'd heard of the legend all the way from the Highlands. Life is stranger than fiction sometimes. "I take it the wife's maiden name is Hatfield?"

She nodded. "Sara Hatfield. She kept it after marrying Danny."

I keyed in the name and retrieved the phone number. In seconds someone had taken our confirmed reservation. Hell, I could buy the hotel if that helped, but I wasn't going to give that game away anytime soon, considering how she felt about those she thought of as having too much money. Strange attitude, considering how important money was to the flow of things.

"We're good to go. I think we should head there tonight, soon as you can close up." I tucked my phone in my pocket. "We'll also need the names and home addresses of the people on the tour."

"I have all that on file. But Sara Hatfield knows me. I'll need to disguise myself. Wear a wig and different clothes."

"Good thinking. When we leave here, we'll swing by the show and find something for you to wear. There are all kinds of wigs and outfits in the costume department."

"Who do you think did it?" she asked.

"I think at the moment we can't rule anyone out. But in my opinion the two elderly sisters are a long shot. The ghost hunter was also very busy and not likely to care one way or another, though it would be a good disguise. The man in the fedora, the tall thin goth guy and the young hipster, all three are prime suspects."

"That's what I'm thinking too."

"See, we're already a great team," I said, enjoying pointing it out. "This case will be solved in no time." Even if I had to drag each of those men into my lair and beat the living tar out of them. And with my forebears loving to raid the countryside for cattle and women, and not necessarily in that order, I had a fairly decent DNA code to rest my case upon.

"How long do we have before they figure out I have a beef with the victim? It makes me look guilty," she said, a quaver in her voice as a nervous tic began under her right eye.

I was at her side in an instant. "Don't worry. It's all going to work out just fine."

"You can't be certain of that." She shrugged off my reassurance and the arm I placed around her shoulders.

"You don't think we're smarter, more charismatic and definitely better-looking than the detectives, my gorgeous, brilliant, soon-to-be assistant?" I dead-panned.

She laughed nervously. We both knew the stakes couldn't be higher. Her freedom was on the line. Between her track record with the law and her dispute with the victim, the cops would be digging into her as a suspect more than anyone else in that death room. So this was the threat that Cristaldo referred to. Everything made sense now, falling into alignment.

I had to solve this, in no small way to pay back my boon to the House of Luceres, but mostly because I cared that Esme live her life free of the stain of being a suspect in a murder investigation. She already carried the burden of public shaming over her need to debunk frauds and bore the trauma of her parents' skewed view of the world that had so deeply affected her. I admired her though, for trying to call out frauds, if not her methods of doing so.

"Well, I know I am," she quipped back. "But what are you?"

Now it was my turn to laugh out loud at the immaturity of the silly taunt. I had guaranteed to protect her, even from herself, and this I vowed to do.

No matter what it took…

Chapter Eight

Esme

"No way am I dressing like a...a hooker! Get that idea right out of that devious mind of yours right now, Mr. Lachlan Creig! If you're such a mind reader, you'd know that." I cringed at the idea of wearing what he had outstretched in my direction, clinging to his hands. A stretchy red lace number that would highlight every curve and expose my religion, as my southern belle of a grandmother would say.

"Never said I'm a mind reader. A ghost reader would be more accurate. And" — he waved the tiny bit of cloth in front of my face — "you did say you wanted to look entirely different. That sackcloth you're wearing is not going to change up anything, even with that adorable curly red wig."

I touched the wig with reverence. I'd always wanted to be a vivacious redhead like my friend and partner at Ghoststompers, Inc., Meghan Hilton, a shifter from the

Canadian Shield pack who felt as much an outsider as me. And now I had the perfect excuse to emulate those coveted curls that flowed so beautifully down her back to her waist in wild abandon. A Lady Godiva look-a-like if there ever was one, and her family even raised horses. She'd barrel raced as a teenager and had the medals and ribbons to prove it.

I pushed aside outfit after outfit on the long rack, each one more scandalous than the last. "Okay, I can't do this. You chose — there's nothing here less than too revealing."

He handed me the bit of red lace, managing the feat without so much as a smirk. I would have loved to know more about what the man was thinking under that façade of impassive strength, as alpha as I had ever experienced in any of the Roman Houses that existed in Vegas. Something deeper lived under his surface magnificence, his charm, something that called to me and gave me pause. It kept me guessing and intrigued, beyond the physical attraction.

"You change and I'll pick out some more dresses. It might take a few days to solve this case and you don't want to be caught wearing the same thing twice. I have female relatives who share those facts straight up."

I groaned and slipped into the dressing room. Taking off the period costume with some difficulty, I breathed a sigh of relief to be free of the heavy fabric. Being around Lachlan was making me a hot, perspiring mess with my damn hormones running wild, but I recognized his assistance would be useful. Maybe if we did have sex, it would lower the attraction factor down to bearable levels? At least it would help me manage until we could go our separate ways so I could catch my damn breath again.

I tugged the red lace dress over my hips, trying not to tear the fragile fabric, shaking my head at what the form-fitting garment did to my body. Then I slipped into the matching stilettos that could double as awesome weapons. But I did like the wig and adjusted the lovely curls that I could never manage with my own poker-straight fine hair. No one I knew would recognize me now, looking more like an upscale hooker about to enter a penthouse suite at a high-class hotel. Well, this would certainly help the insane attraction between me and uber-wolf. *Not.*

A part of me was smirking at the look I was certain was about to appear on his ridiculously handsome face, so I pushed the curtain aside and stepped from the cramped dressing room, posing with a hand on my hip like celebrities do on the red carpet.

I was not disappointed. His chiseled jaw tightened almost measurably, his intense eyes lighting up with bursts of green fire. His large hands twitched ever so slightly, his kilt pushed outward and my one coherent thought was, *Run for your life, Esme.*

I swallowed. Should I heed my own advice? Looking around the space, I didn't know which way would be best to make a break for it, not having paid enough attention coming in. Between the insane attraction to Lachlan and needing to solve a murder mystery, my mind was a little preoccupied. But my whole body was riveted now, watching the huge alpha wolf look at me like he wanted to devour me.

"Aw, everything okay?" I asked, sliding my hand ever so slowly down my side, not certain if I should move at all. This would be an awesome occasion to be able to shift. Well, maybe I'd escape, but as his wolf would no doubt prove as powerful as him, I couldn't imagine being able to get away. The urge to join him on a run through the desert rose, overwhelming my defenses. Would I ever find my own Forever Mate, because if I did and we shared the right DNA, there was a good chance I could shift one day. *Choose wrong and it might never happen.* It was a fragile hope at best.

I licked my dry lips nervously, still frozen in place. His gaze dropped to watch the action. Then he was on the move, stalking straight for me, and the craziest part was I didn't want to escape. Not once he laid his strong hands on me, drawing me close to that awesome six-pack. His warmth was my undoing.

He picked me up in his arms then and pressed hard against me, his kisses landing all over my face, the suddenness knocking my wig off. I didn't care, just brought up my legs to hug his slim waist as he ravaged my mouth, seeking the warmth inside. Rockets fired off in my mind, my panties instantly soaking wet. I ached for him, not believing that any attraction could be this strong. This had to be some kind of heavenly magic voodoo.

"*Mo leannan*, the things being around you does to me," he murmured between kisses that stirred my flesh as he called me his lover, with each press of his warm lips waking all my longings to be with a man. *This man.*

The loud slam of a door shattered the moment. *Crap.* Someone was coming.

Lachlan didn't let me go, but I knew he heard when he brought up his head to snag glances with me. His golden-brown locks framed his face and I reached up to tuck one behind his ear. His hair was as soft as it looked, silky to the touch. I itched to run my hands through it, then run my fingers all over his fine, strong hunk of a body.

"Hush," he said. "Maybe they'll go away."

In the quiet moment we waited as one, his heart beating soundly against my breasts. Then footsteps echoed, coming closer. It sounded like two different sets of boots striding across the floor.

He grimaced and slid me slowly down his body until my feet touched the floor. All the way down with that thick cock touching me. *Every. Square. Inch of the way.* I longed to grab it and put it to good use. Instead, I picked up the wig from the floor, slipping it back on. Best to stay disguised. Though I didn't think anything would hide my high color or obvious arousal.

I pressed my thighs together and wished the acute ache would leave, give me some freakin' peace. Humping Lachlan's leg might be considered unladylike, but right then, at that moment in time, I wished instant attraction was a damn myth for werewolves, whether they could shift or not.

Because if this kept up, I was going to lose my damn mind.

Chapter Nine

Lachlan

Who dared to interrupt? The two detectives came into view, both looking too grim and serious. Both sets of eyes widened at the sight of Esme in her new outfit. I could not hold back a warning growl.

Stay away. She's mine.

A direct threat to Esme stood before us. I stepped in front of her to shield her from view.

"I thought we'd find you both here," Detective Tom Olson said before giving his partner Sam Jackson a look of meaning, like he'd won some kind of bet. "It's come to my attention that Esme didn't share a pertinent fact important to the case. Is it true, Miss Luceres, that Danny McCoy refused to pay your company for the ghost-hunting work you did for him?"

"How did you get in?" I demanded. I wanted to toss both of them out on their ears.

"We had the night watchman let us in. Badges speak volumes in our town. But you haven't answered the question. Did Danny McCoy ever pay you what you were owed for the job?"

"You don't have to answer that, Esme," I said, putting out a hand to keep her behind me.

"I can speak for my damn self!" she said, thwarting my best efforts to protect her. She pulled away from me and stood by my side, arms over her chest while I had to stamp out the idea of picking her up in *my* arms and racing for the Highlands to keep her safe.

"You should know that we've already checked everyone's social media sites and it seems one of your cohorts has posted about the hotel not bothering to pay you. Sounded like someone…possibly the owner…was quite put out about it."

"If you know that, why are you bothering me?" she demanded. "It means nothing anyway because I had *nothing* to do with what occurred earlier. I was kept busy trying to do my job, meaning I had less time than anyone else to be up to anything nefarious. You should be checking out the others. I was under the most scrutiny of any of them the entire time. Hosting a tour does require one to be the center of attention, Detective."

"It doesn't take but a split second to inject someone," Detective Olson said. "Especially as it was crowded and dark in that attic."

"The husband was with someone half his age. Is the wife involved in some way? When I spent nights there, they were too busy fighting to care all that much about what I was up to. Jealousy's a powerful motive, Detective," Esme said.

"Do you know for certain that poison was involved? Hardly time for an autopsy report to be concluded. It seems all this speculation is rather premature," I said, even though I had mentioned it first. It was murder, but they didn't *know* that yet. Why were they at this again so soon? I'd have it solved for them in no time. They could go home and party for all it mattered. *Leave us the hell alone.*

"We'll know soon enough. It's my job to make sure we have all the facts. Seems you're rather more interested in hampering the investigation, Mr. Creig. Any reason for that?" Detective Olson asked, his expression hardening.

Anger seethed through my veins at the memory of another case detectives bungled—deep anger that turned the room red. Police stupidity had given a stalker carte blanche to continue his evil ways...*and look at the tragedy that occurred and tore our family apart.* I shook my head, trying to wipe away the torturous image of Mary, my cousin's Forever Mate, dead in his arms.

"And you, Mr. Creig, it turns out, have no license to operate as a lawyer in the state of Nevada."

"I will be hiring the best team available in this country to see that you cease and desist from annoying Miss Luceres any further. Are we clear?" My expression convinced the two men to take a step backward before sharing another glance with each other. "And for the record, Miss Luceres does not have to say another word to you without her lawyer present," I added for good measure.

"No need to get riled. We'll see ourselves out, but neither of you are to leave town. Understood?"

I glared at them the entire time they hurried away from us, shooting flames into their backs. It was odd they didn't experience spontaneous combustion.

"I could have handled them. I don't know what women are like in your country, but I can do things for myself. You didn't need to antagonize them like that, Lachlan," Esme confronted me.

"You need my help, *mo leannan*, and you will have it. It's for your own good."

"My own good! I can hire my own lawyer if it comes to that, which it won't, since I'm not guilty."

What was it with females? *Two steps forward, then one back.* She was being difficult about something that required iron control. This was why I usually avoided spending time with the female sex!

I pulled out my phone, turning my back on Esme. I could feel her fuming and frustrated as she waited while I texted the words necessary to bring a team of help to descend on the city. I wasn't taking chances with Esme—if I had to, I'd put her in a sterile bubble to keep her safe. She'd understand in time that my actions only had her best interests at heart.

"Okay, we need to head to the hotel now," I said at last.

"I'm not going with you!"

"What are you on about? Of course, you are. I'm the only one that can keep you safe." Flummoxed, I could only stare at her.

"Not until I've had my say. We need to work this out. I'm not a damsel in distress. I spend long nights in haunted houses without incident. I can handle myself. I know karate moves, self-defense moves, and I'm licensed to pack a gun when necessary. And damn it, Lachlan, I'm a Luceres with all the strengths that brings

84

to the table. Just because I can't shift, that doesn't mean I'm helpless or less than."

Her expression changed at that moment and my heart squeezed. Not being able to shift bothered her a great deal. So this was where some of her rash actions originated? At that moment I learned a lot about Esme, feeling closer to her.

"No one would ever say that you're less than, *mo leannan*. Just because you aren't shifting yet, doesn't mean that's forever. My cousin's wife couldn't shift until she married her Forever Mate. Sharing DNA allowed her to shift, with practice. Perhaps it will be the same for you."

She swiped at her eyes, now brightening with hope. She looked away from me as if she felt too vulnerable after spilling the insecurity of not living up to being a proper shifter.

"Okay, let's get out of here. Sooner we solve this damn thing, the better," she said, picking up the suitcase of dresses I'd chosen for her and striding away from me toward the exit. I'd taken the liberty of texting my man Alistair to prepare the penthouse suite at the hotel with everything we might need. Alistair was a godsend who kept my life in good order and headed up the small army of people required to arrange things to run smoothly for my gigs in Vegas. He'd be happy to do the same work for Esme with what I paid him. Well, if the fiery beauty would let him.

I let out a deep breath. Maybe I was learning something about how to handle females after all. I'd always been accused of being cold. One-night stands had become a specialty, something I wasn't proud of. But seeing the pain my cousin had experienced over losing Mary had left it a little hard to leave myself open going forward.

Chapter Ten

Esme

I decided to hang back a bit while Lachlan booked us into the Hatfield & McCoy hotel. Loki was part of the package, and he sat obediently at my side. I liked having him around, a huge dog that would drive away any predator. Actually, I knew where he got that attitude from, I thought, looking over at his master as he took charge of things. But it was still best not to tempt fate and let anyone get too good a look at me, though all the female clerk's bowing and scraping over Lachlan was annoying.

The spacious lobby featured framed black-and-white photographs from the era. The two large families involved in the feud after the Civil War were captured standing or sitting outside their respective old log cabins. There was also historical paraphernalia of gunslingers, six-shooters and a map of the sections of Kentucky and West Virginia that the two families controlled and fought over, killing a number of clansmen over the years.

It had been a tragic state of affairs in which people lost their lives, so it was good to see the feud had eventually played itself out. The two families had even gotten together for a reunion at the turn of the millennium, and the smiling group of hundreds of family members concluded the interesting display. *Families should get along, stick together.* Maybe I was being too hard on my family by always ducking and dodging every attempt to bring me closer to the fold?

"All set," Lachlan said, joining us.

"Great." I noted the raised eyebrows of the clerk, who was taking in my state of dress. I tugged at the hem of my skirt, wishing for a bit more fabric to magically appear.

"You look gorgeous, Esme. Flaunt it while you have it, The Creig always says." Lachlan placed a warm arm about my shoulders, directing me to the bank of elevators. Now that we were there, I had sudden concerns about the sleeping arrangements. No way could I avoid making a huge mistake and riding Lachlan's considerable assets if we slept in too close proximity. And with the police hot on my trail, why was *that* my first worry? A frisson of unease crept down my spine, making me shiver. What if someone or something else pointed a finger at me? What then? I had to solve this ASAP. The bet with Lachlan aside, this was my life we were talking about here. A clock began ticking loudly in my head.

"You okay, *m'eudail*?" Lachlan asked, obviously noting my shiver.

"Yeah." I had to admit, I was enjoying all the sweet terms he used in that wonderous deep baritone of his more than I should.

He pushed the button for the penthouse suite and the elevator ascended smoothly to the eighth floor, low by Vegas standards, but still a money-maker. Hmm, money…did that have something to do with it? Was the wife worried about Danny divorcing her and taking a huge chunk of the assets? Maybe she'd even hired a private eye to check up on him. It wasn't like he was really hiding the affair.

"What's Danny's current wife's name?" Lachlan asked as we left the elevator, him carrying my suitcase.

"Sara. And she was his second wife. Maybe there was a pre-nuptial agreement and the wife stands to lose more than she thinks fair?"

"I'll tell the lawyers to look into that."

"Lawyers. What lawyers?" I turned on him, then noted he wasn't looking me in the eyes at the moment.

Lachlan

"I'm making certain your rights are being well taken care of. Just in case. A precaution only."

"I can't afford the best. No way. Disengage them, right now!"

She got that look in her eye that said she was getting pushed too far, too quickly, but I couldn't stop myself. Surely protecting her was the first order of business?

"No. I think that's a mistake, Esme. Besides, the Luceres would expect that I do what an alpha thinks best, standing in their place. I will protect you — that's my code of honor. Nothing else to be said about it. My mind's made up."

"Good grief, Lachlan. Don't you guys ever quit this silly posturing?" she said with a shake of her head. Loki prowled the room, checking everything out before dropping down on the thick rug and watching us. The dog had it easy. He and Esme were already friends.

How to explain? "A woman can fall prey to things she may not expect. You need to be careful, Esme. And if you're not willing to do so with my help, then so help me—"

"What? You'll do what? Throw me in a cage and toss away the key like my uncle did to my aunt thirty years ago? No, this is a new millennium. Things like that don't happen anymore."

"Yes, they do." I would do whatever it took to keep her safe.

She glared at me, her mouth pleated like she was busy making a decision. *And probably not in my favor.*

"If you think for one minute that I will allow you to restrict my movements in any way, you have another think coming. Now, I want my own room, a long, long way from yours. We clear?"

"You are a *gallus* lass for certain. We have the entire top floor. You can sleep as far from me as you want. Just don't expect me to stop my efforts to keep you safe."

"*Gallus.* What does that mean?" She wrinkled her nose in that way I found particularly fetching.

"Overly confident and aggravating." I enjoyed the expression that came over her lovely face. "Also, a term of endearment by some. It's a fine line between confidence and arrogance, Esme."

"You should know. You ride it all the time!"

I caught the smile she was trying to hide. "Why are we fighting when we have a murder to solve? Wouldn't our best energies be directed toward the enemy?" I asked pointedly.

"Yes. Keep your mind on figuring it out and less on how to control me. We'll get along just fine then."

"So you say. I won't apologize for doing what's right." I'd haul her fine ass away to my castle and imprison her in the tower if need be. A new thought jump-started my brain. Oh Lord, was this the legendary mating dance The Creig warned of, the heralding of a Forever Mate? Maybe I should be thinking of protecting my heart now, considering how much her safety meant to me.

"No, but maybe you'll be begging me for a favor and I'll turn you down."

She pranced away after the throwing down of the gauntlet.

The lass was going to be the death of me. I knew it now.

Chapter Eleven

Esme

I didn't know whether to kill him or jump his bones. I was that aggravated and confused. Why on earth was my body driving me to distraction when my brain knew well that there was an important puzzle that must be solved?

Whether I liked it or not, Lachlan was staunchly on my side, making certain I had what I needed to go forward. I just had to help him see that his idea of protecting a female went too far. He needed to let go of the reins, join the modern decade. Maybe it was just a Highlands werewolf thing? No, that wasn't quite right. When my cousins were chasing their Forever Mates, all rules seemed off the table. Crazy stuff happened all the time, like the time the Luceres twins headed all the way to the top of the world to find a legendary artifact that promised to save their mate.

Oh. Crap. Was this something more than a ridiculously insane and beyond the pale attraction between a female and a male?

Take a deep breath, Esme. Lachlan hasn't suggested anything of the kind. In fact, I bet he's got a woman in every port just waiting for their big, bad, handsome werewolf to sail in. Damn it, but I didn't like that view of him either.

I squeezed my head between my hands, standing in the roomy shower and letting the water sluice over my naked body. I needed to go to bed, but my brain was racing. At least I had a private area to one side of the penthouse while Lachlan had set up camp in the other half of the place. We could go days without seeing each other if need be.

Yeah, like that would ever happen. *He doesn't see me at breakfast in the morning and he'll be breaking down the door.* Then he'd be all over me. Lips kissing, hands caressing, that excellent package ready, willing and able, judging by the size of his cock I'd had pressed against me during the kiss at the theater. *Before the cops interrupted. Good thing too.* I might have made the biggest mistake of my life, letting my body take control of things.

A loud knock on the bathroom door broke my concentration.

"You okay in there? You've been in the shower a long time."

I groaned. "Go away. I'm thinking." *Of you, Mr. Lachlan Creig, far too much.*

"Join me when you're done. We need to talk. Make a plan together."

Whether I liked it or not, that was a good idea. "I'll be there in a few minutes. Keep your pants on." *Or not.*

"I look better without them, *m'eudail*."

I laughed, somewhat relieved when I heard him walk away and close the door. I quickly soaped up, feeling the tingle on my sensitive nipples as my hands massaged the bodywash in. *Yes, imagine his long, beautifully formed fingers doing the task for me. His lips descending to grasp a bud in his warm mouth, sucking hard until my clit becomes swollen with desire.* I spread my legs, letting my fingers take over like I wanted Lachlan to do. I pushed two up inside me, a poor substitute for the hard cock I knew existed under that tempting kilt of his. The way he strutted around, enticing a woman to distraction. All bare abs on stage, like a marble statue of an Adonis.

I gasped aloud as I came, dizzy with the overwhelming need to be made love to. Doing it myself may have sucked big-time, but what was a gal to do? Throw herself at him, taking a risk like that she could keep her heart safe? *Bad idea, Esme.*

I quickly dried myself and combed out my wet hair, then donned a thick terry robe the hotel provided in their best suite. There was nothing shabby about the way Lachlan did things. His job at the casino must pay big. Lucky him, having the charisma of a modern-day warrior to boot. Too easy to predict he'd go far with his show.

Having taken the extreme edge off my desire to jump his bones, I exited my end of the top floor and, padding on the thick carpets in my bare feet, went in search of my host.

Lachlan

"Her eyes outshine the radiant beams, That gild the passing shower, And glitter o'er the crystal streams, And cheer each fresh'ning flower."

She was a looker and appeared younger with her radiant face free of makeup. Why did women bother with the stuff? I ached to kiss her and pull the robe off. But I made myself to the right thing, hard as it was and hard as *I* was, and watched her plunk herself down on the loveseat next to me. Her fresh fragrance of cleanliness and flowers filled me with the urge to press my face against her skin, to breathe in her essence.

"Poetry?" She gave me a stunned look. Then she licked her lips. Aye, she liked the bare-chested posture I had assumed, throwing off the restraint of a shirt.

"Robbie Burns, and no other. It's from *Young Peggy*. Burns was a prolific plowman-poet, our resident genius. It's considered essential that a Scotsman memorize some of his verse. No matter if you're a shifter or not."

"I like it. Just surprised, but in a good way. What are you researching?"

I enjoyed the way she cuddled in next to me to observe the computer screen. I took a deeper breath, all the more to appreciate all the more the delicious scent that filled my nostrils. *Jasmine with a feminine musk that made every cell in my body take notice.*

"Checking out all the people that came on the tour. Seems that we have a few prime suspects so far."

"You mean after me?" she said, her smile of confidence a bit wobbly. Loki raised his head at the tremor in her voice, a look of concern for Esme. I gave him a reassuring nod and he lay back down. *I'll take care of it, boy.*

"You didn't do it, no need to worry. But one of the males, Fedora guy—he's got an arrest record, as does ghost man. Fedora's on drugs and weapons charges and ghost man for trespassing on private property. The tall thin goth man's a computer geek without a blemish and doesn't look near as promising, though his get-up bears looking into. Mephistophelian or what?" I chuckled.

"The spinsters are staying right here in this hotel, which has to be investigated further. The millennial is the least likely of all to have committed the crime, a middle-school teacher from the mid-west on vacation. The victim's girlfriend works at a nightclub as a dancer, which opens another avenue of interest. The Blue Bayou has a notorious reputation," I added.

She punched my arm. "You don't know they're spinsters. Could you find any connection between Fedora guy or ghost man and Danny McCoy?"

"Nothing definitive as yet. Ghost man works at a Staples during the day, which needs checking out. Fedora guy's staying at the Pink & Glo Flamingo, a seedy joint off the Strip. I've got someone watching the place to make sure he doesn't check out since he's from out of town."

"You already hired a private investigator?"

"I've hired a *team* of private investigators, who are considered the best, most discreet operators in the business."

She narrowed her eyes at me. "I never asked you to do that! I thought we were going to solve this together? How much is this going to cost me? I'm not rolling in dough and I *never* ask my relatives for handouts. It's called freedom and independence." She pulled away from me and began pacing around the living room.

"What's money for if not to spend, *caileag ghrinn*?"

"What does *caileag ghrinn* mean? I understood some of the others, but that one's new."

"Lovely lass, and truer words were never spoken. Esme, you need my help. I'm not saying I'm as rich as

Midas," I lied, "but comfortable enough to make sure all the facts are exposed in this case. It's often not being innocent or guilty that sends a person to jail, but how much money they have to spend to prove themselves innocent of the crime."

"That's a rather jaded view of the justice system." She stopped pacing and faced me.

"You're saying no innocent person has ever been kept behind bars? Or guilty person been set free?" I shook my head. I'd been told I had a stone heart by others, mainly women, who thought my views were hard and too world-weary. Well, I'd learned that it was best to never leave anything up to others to do. Mary would still be alive if justice had been done. *If she had been protected properly by the law.*

I never spoke of what had happened to Mary to anyone. Our family had pulled a veil over it. Sometimes I wondered if it wouldn't have been better to get it more out in the open, talk about it. If not put it behind us, at least make some peace with it.

Esme looked more indecisive now, her brows pulling together as she chewed on a fingernail. I preferred her spirited, but I also wanted her safe more. Could there not be a compromise?

"Fine, but I'm paying you back every cent that it costs. Are we clear? I'm not a damn charity case!"

"If you insist." *Over my dead body you'll pay for anything.* Some things a man or wolf does not compromise on. "Now, let's have a drink and put our feet up." I poured two snifters from my own private stock that Alistair had been instructed to bring, the Macallan Lalique, a fifty-year-old single malt Scotch whiskey, the pride of Speyside in the Highlands of Scotland. The cost of a bottle would pay for the entire investigation. What was the point of not enjoying the fruits of labor?

The urge to haul her back to Castle Creigbourne was pulling at my mortal soul, but that would have to wait until her name was cleared and she was free of any whiff of scandal. That would be the first order of business.

She took an appreciative sip, her eyes lighting up. "Unbelievably smooth. I don't think I've tasted better. Where did this come from?"

"Are you saying a Highlander can't have eclectic tastes, *caileag ghrinn*?"

She blushed, her creamy skin firm and peachlike. I craved to touch her again, to breathe in her fragrance. "Of course not. But my family enjoys high-end spirits, especially the Luceres brothers that run the Glitter Palace, and I wondered if they had ever drunk it?" She set her drink down after another sip. "Talking about the Luceres…"

"Yes." I could see the questions in her eyes. I had to be extra careful, not let out anything about my interactions with Cristaldo. "What is it you want to know?"

"I've really not paid much attention to other groups of werewolves up till now. Kind of annoyed, I guess because…well, the reason doesn't matter. But I'd like to know more about where you come from, Lachlan? Your ancestry?"

"*Ma's breug bh' uam e, is breug dhomh e.* If it be a lie as told by me, it was a lie as told to me. An expression oft used by The Creig, my grandmother, who shared the second sight with me, the first born of our family." I finished my dram of liquor, poured myself a second glass and topped hers off.

"Go on. I'd love to hear more about The Creig and your family," Esme said, tucking her feet under herself. The action let the robe gap open at the neckline and the view of the tops of her creamy breasts made my mouth water. I had to look away to answer. My wolf was on high alert, ready to pounce at the slightest provocation.

"She's a lot like you, with plenty of spunk to spare."

The image brought another smile to Esme's face and I savored a rare moment with her.

"It would be lovely to meet her. She sounds right up my alley. What do your parents do?"

"Well, you could say they run a B & B on *Eilean maddah-allaidh* or Wolf Island, in the Highlands to the west of Scotland." *Not* totally *a lie...* "It's gorgeous there, one of the most geologically diverse landmasses in the world. Hauntingly beautiful. The view from the cas..." I stopped myself mid-sentence.

"Sounds amazing." She didn't push it further, sensitive to my reticence. "Please, tell me more about the history of your clan."

"As you wish. Eighth century early enough for you?"

She nodded, her expression rapt.

"We mated with and added Viking blood to our Highland Wulver Clans during the invasions of Scotland back in the eighth century. Changed our name to Highland Heathens at that time. We're a powerful mix of the Viking wolf Fenrir that heralds the end of the world during the Ragnarök, and warrior blood, impossible to beat on the battlefield."

Her eyes popped open. "That's some awesome lineage. Rivals the three Houses of Luceres, Anche and Ribelle begun during the founding of Rome about the same time your clans were encountering the Viking raids. The myth of Romulus and Romulus...all a reality for our race. The Lupus Sanguis Chalice that can save a werewolf's life, made from the bone and blood of the original wolf, came from that era."

"We are both from powerful clans, Esme, the best in the world."

The richest too, which was not a failing at all, apart from what the lass thought of it. But I could only imagine the offspring such a union would create. A legacy yet to be earned. The moment was potent, my second sight kicking into high gear like a crack opening in creation, through which I was given a profound image of the future. One that struck fear into my heart if I didn't get things right.

But now I knew exactly what I was dealing with, and why I was so drawn to Esme.

Chapter Twelve

Esme

Lachlan's expression tightened as he stilled, his eyes, normally so bright green and intense, shifted to a lighter shade, then almost bleached to white. A couple of worrying seconds later his eyes returned to their normal brightness, though his expression remained grim.

"What is it? Did you see something? Was that the second sight?" I pounced on him, needing to know everything. Now.

"Nothing to worry about. Are you hungry?"

"No." *At least not for food.* But he was hiding something from me. I could press harder, but I sensed it would do me little good. Better to sleep on all this and have at it in the morning? That was about my most mature thought. Maybe. Ever. Certainly around Lachlan anyway.

"I should be going," I said, setting down my empty glass for emphasis. The delicious heat from the liquor curled warmly in my stomach, relaxing me. I got to my feet and swayed slightly. In a flash, Lachlan had his arms around me.

His half-naked body was too much for me to handle. My defenses depleted from the day, I ended up clinging to him, breathing in a fragrance of heather and musk that ensnared me to him. I savored the moment, but it was too soon. If we hit the sheets now, how would I face myself in the morning? A quick tryst in the bed where so many other women had probably been before me? Just not going to happen. I couldn't lay myself open to such heartbreak.

But the thinking no and the saying no were not the same thing.

And his body and mine were absolutely beyond-a-shadow-of-doubt certain they wanted to connect at the most elementary level. *Hold on, think this through, Esme.* It was a bad idea to mix business with pleasure. Or maybe the best idea I ever had if I wanted to escape for a while? But then what? We'd be uncomfortable with each other and still have a murder to solve.

Finally, I found the strength to say it. "No, I don't want to be just another notch on your belt, Lachlan." Being with such a man then losing him when he didn't need my help anymore because the case was solved was too painful to consider.

"What's this about?" he asked, his expression thunderous, his displeasure breaking through his normally calm demeanor. Beneath that awesome exterior lived passion and, I suspected, a big heart. "You could never be that. You are a Luceres."

"Is that what you want, a Luceres? Because with me, you don't get full access to them. I'll always be the outsider."

"I don't need them or their connections at all. I am a Heathen, a Wulver, an ancient warrior. And you are so much more than a Luceres to me, *caileag ghrinn.*"

I pulled away from him, welcome as his words were. "It's late. I need to go."

He was too much a gentleman to restrain me, though I saw the flash of power in his eyes that suggested it cost him not to just throw me over his shoulder and bear me to bed. Or onto the floor. Maybe I wanted that? To feel that undeniable attraction of his having to be with me so badly he didn't worry about taking chances. *Crazy thought.* That was a fantasy for novels, not real-world stuff. I couldn't possibly want that, could I?

Actually, I was so wanting this guy, so filled with lust, I could imagine throwing *him* over my shoulder if I were capable. He was twice my size and probably many times my strength, so not going to happen this century.

Lachlan's eyes darkened to glittering emeralds. He took a deep breath, filling those amazing lungs with air. Magic surrounded us, pulsating with a surplus of energy that would only take a spark to catch fire. My lust was communicating to him on every level.

Time to run like hell.

I turned and raced for the doorway, headed for my hoped-to-be-off-limits part of the penthouse. I should know better than to run from a wolf. That was She-wolf 101. Basic intel that even a twelve-year-old would know.

I almost made it. Loki growled in warning.

"Stand down, boy. It's fine." Lachlan reassured the giant dog.

His big brawny hands grasped me around the waist and sent a shiver of excitement through my entire system, his body so close to mine. His voice, dropped to the deepest timbre, threatened to capsize the best of intentions.

"Hold on, Esme. I don't want you to think for one moment that I would ever see you but in the best of light. We've met in the oddest circumstances, I'll give you that...but I respect where you're coming from. Much as I want to bed you, and I do want that, I want you to be ready for me. For us."

This wasn't at all what I expected.

Exposed.

Taken.

Ravished.

That was the vision in my mind. I blushed to the very tips of my toes as realization hit home. Lachlan might well be my Forever Mate, judging by the insane attraction. And if he was, the whole world might open up for me. Because what I felt for him was far too much to be normal. It was off-the-charts insane. But if this was only lust and nothing more, and being with him wouldn't break my heart when he moved on, then maybe I could let myself go for once? Be with a man just because I desired him more than anything else on earth at that moment?

"Oh, Lachlan, why now, why you?" I heard the quaking tremor in my own voice. "Why are you driving me to distraction? Why do I want to make love to you so badly my very soul hurts from the wanting?"

His eyes widened with my revelation. "Something is going on between us that defies explanation."

"I'm afraid. Afraid that we'll catch fire and I'll be lost. Burned to cinders."

"Making love? No harm ever came from that. That's where you *find* yourself, not *lose* yourself. Always been the way of it. The nature of the beast that cannot be stopped. That's the immortal part of us, connected to the universe."

"No, it's too soon," I said, pulling away. It all sounded too much, with too much riding on it.

I took the opportunity his lessened grip provided, striding from the room. I threw my robe off behind closed doors, too heated to bear its touch on my sensitive flesh. I needed an output for my aggravation, my pent-up lust, my need for control.

Damn it, if only I could shift to a wolf, I could run and run and run and never look back. Was a noose tightening around my neck? A terrible picture formed in my head and I put my hand to my throat, wondering where in the hell that idea had come from. No, there were no ghosts in this hotel. No haunting entity that could send me such a horrifying image.

A clock was ticking in the room, very loud. Too loud. *Tick-tock. Tick-tock.* It seemed to echo from the very walls themselves. I was overtired and overwrought — that was all this was, a flight of fantasy. But how on earth was I to sleep worked up to the nines?

Impossible.

Chapter Thirteen

Lachlan

I paced back and forth in my side of the penthouse. My flesh burned. I needed to be with her. Not just because my cock was hard enough to burst, but because of wanting to be with *her*, that exciting, witty, passionate, vulnerable woman I had gotten to know in the past few days, one who cared enough to put herself at risk for others.

I wanted to know more about her, so much more. Since that first vision back on *Eilean maddah-allaidh*, everything had been about finding blue eyes and golden hair, of finding Esme. I had no doubts now. And she wanted me just as bad as I wanted her. That was beyond obvious. Her scent trail had buried itself inside me, left me raw for only her.

What was stopping her? I'd had women fall into my bed within five minutes of meeting, for heaven's sake. We were both created from origin myths, the stuff of legends. Destined to walk this world as the chosen, abilities without parallel. What was keeping us from following the natural progression of male and female shifter?

Maybe it was this damn murder investigation that was getting in our way?

My phone rang. "Lachlan here," I growled into the annoying device, having discovered I disliked being interrupted while thinking about Esme.

"Lachlan, it's Calan. Just letting you know that Logan and I will be there for Friday night's show, two days from now, and we're bringing along a big group. Twenty-five in total are itching to come and see the magnificent magician in action. I told them they'd have to make do with the likes of you." Calan chuckled, enjoying the dig.

"Maybe you're not seeking a backstage pass like the others then, since you think you're making do? That will save some trouble," I said. The clock that had been ticking loudly these past few hours couldn't get louder. My worry over Esme topped everything else.

Calan continued, his tone far more contrite, "Aww, you're making twenty-four passes anyway, what's one more? We should be there in plenty of time to catch up with you before the show. The Creig says she'd rather be coming to Vegas for her grandson's wedding, but she's still looking forward to seeing you."

"Sounds like The Creig." The support of my two brothers wouldn't go amiss, not to mention that of a mishmash of aunts, uncles and cousins. But that meant I had less than forty-eight hours to solve the mystery if I wanted to keep the news from my clan. And that, I badly wanted, preferring not even a whiff of the trouble make its way to any of their ears. The proud Creigs would be outraged by the accusation. *No telling what some of them might do.* The idea sent more aggravation straight to my brain. At least it took my mind off another body part.

"What's up, bro? You sound off to me. A bit more growly than usual."

"It's a woman."

Calan snickered. "Isn't it always?"

"It's not like that." A wave of anger sliced through me. *Calm down.*

"Hmm, what seems to be the trouble? Not preforming to expectations in bed?"

"You know better than that, laddie."

"Sorry, okay, you're serious. I see that now. I should go. You know more about these things than I do," Calan backpedaled.

"You best prepare to catch that plane," I advised.

"We're flying one of our own, so our schedule's flexible. See you soon, Lachlan. Looking forward to meeting your lass as much as The Creig is, I'm certain," Calan said in a respectful tone, befitting a younger sibling.

She already knows. "Don't be spilling this to anyone else yet, Calan. Consider yourself warned."

"Okay, okay. Stay calm. I understand. My lips are sealed. I won't breathe a word of this."

I bid my brother a safe trip then dropped the phone on the table. I took a deep breath. Having Esme so close by was pure torture. I picked up on her every nuance. Her fragrance wafted through the space, seeming stronger and more potent by the second. Every rustle in the bedroom next door made my wolf paw at the floor, desperate to be released.

An intense vision struck hard as I paced the floor, stopping me mid-stride. Hard enough to make me sway, and it was instantly followed by the bright gold and blue of earlier revelations. Only this one was much more specific.

Now. It has to be now!

Chapter Fourteen

Esme

Damn it, I can't sleep! All I could feel was Lachlan pacing in the room next to mine. I swore I could *taste* him, like my body knew it was going to enjoy every single moment with him. Imagining those huge manly hands touching me all over, caressing and pinching and sucking... I just about fainted from the overwhelming heat that set in between my legs. This was the true meaning of torture. If his cock wasn't headed inside me in the next few minutes, I was going to expire. They would find nothing but cinders in the morning.

If this is what it's like to find my Forever Mate, I want out. As far away from here as possible. I was losing my damn mind. I pressed my hand to my mound once again, trying to relieve the acute pressure. Nothing worked. One orgasm just led to another beginning, another throbbing. An endless cycle of need with no relief in sight.

That's it!

I leaped off the bed and ran bare-ass naked to the door, then flung it wide open. Lachlan faced me, his handsome face and incredible body taunting me. He was a gladiator, an ancient warrior, his golden aura jerking my strings like I was a damn puppet.

"It's now or never, Lachlan!"

"My pleasure, *caileag ghrinn*. I thought you'd never ask." His movements were so sudden that my breath hitched. Once second over there by the loveseat, the next pulling me tightly into his brawny arms.

Oh my, when he held me against the searing heat and iron strength of his huge body, every last objection melted into a puddle of need. With reverence, I ran my hands through his dark silky hair, letting the long waves flow through my fingers.

He touched me the same way, running his fingers through the thick strands of my fair hair.

"So soft," he murmured. His dark eyes were pools of liquid, so deep they touched a chord inside my mortal soul.

Now that the consent had been given, the line crossed, we indulged each other, touching and exploring each other's face and body with utter fascination. Like it was the first time that a man and woman, wolf and she-wolf, had encountered the other. The first male and female ever, standing proud and naked together.

"Esme, you're so beautiful. So perfect." He ran his fingers down my face, like a blind man trying to explore and memorize every nook and cranny. With such gentleness that my heart squeezed with joy, he pressed kisses to my face, working his way toward my lips.

When our mouths touched, our tongues seeking entry, I moaned with pleasure, pressing harder against him. My nipples tightened, my pussy clenched with need and the acute fragrance of arousal filled the room to overflowing.

"I want to kiss you all over. Lie down for me," Lachlan demanded in his deep baritone, bearing me up in his arms and depositing me on the bed. He grabbed my ankles and tugged my legs apart, apparently enjoying the view, judging by the wide smile that flashed across that achingly handsome face. He looked timeless to me, a man who had arrived at my doorstep across the centuries, his body carved from the pride of ancient lineage.

He kissed the bottom of my foot, then, ever so slowly, kissed my calf, the delicate space behind my knee, then my thigh. I squirmed, wanting him to get to the main course. He gave a wicked grin. "I said all over, Esme. No part of you will be left to mourn the lack of lovemaking."

He pressed his mouth to the join at the top of my leg and I quit breathing all together, knowing what was coming next. His kisses slowly moved over toward my mound. His fingers joined his mouth as he gently pulled my pussy lips apart before dragging his tongue down the length of my channel. *Oh. My. Goddess.*

The moment was suspended as he kept up the pressure, his tongue amazingly talented. Then he nibbled on my clit and I bucked off the bed, an instant orgasm arcing through me with the speed and power of lightning, making me tremble uncontrollably.

But it wasn't nearly enough, for immediately I wanted more. So much more from him. It was not like this in the past. Was I in heat? I wanted him to fuck me so hard that I was beyond being able to do anything but what pressed at me to do. *Mate. Now.*

"I need you inside me. Now, Lachlan!" I urged with the agony of waiting. Another orgasm tore through me and I shook so wildly that he grabbed my shoulders. Then, as soon as it eased, it began again. Wave after wave of acute throbbing centered in my pussy, a vibration felt so deeply inside that it went straight to the heart of me.

His eyes widened and we locked glances. He knew this was not normal. Beyond the ken. Finally, he took pity on me and without preamble, pushed his huge, thick, hot cock into me, sending it deep inside, right to my core.

I pressed hard with my hands on his ass, my every instinct focused on our joining. Over and over, he slammed into my soaking wet pussy, opening new sensations of pleasure with each push that kept topping the one before. In seconds we were as one. His body my body, my body his.

The joining between my legs was not the only one. It was if we were truly one entity, one soul. So tightly bound there was no going back. Minutes, then hours might have passed, and still we made love, needing the coupling as much as our next breath. We had no control over time or space, just the constant urge to be together. To be as one. Over and over. Lachlan poured his hot seed into me where we were locked together, thrumming with pleasure, and I took it all. And wanted more.

When he swelled and became bigger yet inside me, I could not have escaped the pounding even if I had wanted to, and still I urged him onward. The best meal I'd ever eaten, the most beautiful sunset I'd ever witnessed, the sweetest music I'd ever heard — nothing came close to this, this primal urge to control the beast...*be* the beast. This was the gift of my ancestors.

The gift of the wolf.

Chapter Fifteen

Lachlan

"I need you now, Lachlan!"

The fire in her eyes as she stood naked in the doorway. The scent and signals and need to respond all drew me to her side in an instant. I had to have her. And when she said now, all creation opened up. *Yes.* Forever Esme.

I had to touch her, to experience every part of her. Savor the touch of her sweet body, caress every curve. My very existence depended upon it. The need to ravish her body with my hands and cock, yes, even to procreate and have her bear my young, all flew through my heated brain in an instant as I stepped toward her. No going back. She was mine. My destiny.

Mine.

I kissed her all over, reveling in the fact that such a beautiful woman wanted me as much as I wanted her. When I laid her down on the bed, she opened for me, the view of her wet sweet pink pussy almost too much. But I wanted to give her pleasure first, prepare her for the utter size of my cock.

When she couldn't stand to wait any longer for our union, I saw the truth in her eyes demanding I take her now. *No going back.* I would swell so large inside her that we'd become one. Every fibre of our beings on fire for the other, every moment a sweet torture of victory.

The moment I thrust my cock into her, the room vibrated with the energy of resounding drums. Around the fire, my ancestors beat in rhythm, an ancient song to celebrate a powerful union of alpha and female.

Over and over, I thrust into her, sending my scent deep into every part of her. I had her full permission — her every movement and glance proved it. When she moaned with pleasure, her head thrashing about, I howled aloud, my wolf celebrating the need to claim.

"Do you want it all, Esme?" I asked, being clear about my intentions. Why bother to wait? I knew what I wanted.

"Yes, yes, take all of me. So good..."

Her permission fired my brain and body. I bit her on the shoulder, sending my essence so deep inside her that no one would ever be able to get it out. *Mine. Forever.*

And so the deed was done.

"Did you just bite me?" she asked, her eyes becoming focused for the first time in hours. I smiled at her, still inside her, my cock too large and swollen to remove. I never wanted to move — locked inside her forever was looking better and better.

"Aye, it's the claiming. What you wanted, what your whole body was begging for, my lovely mate."

"What! I wasn't begging for anything." Her expression was priceless. She was as good at being a vixen as the best of them. I could see endless days playing and mating with her. I just had one thing to clear up first.

"No, then who else was it that screamed for me to be with them?" I teased, nipping at her pebbled nipple, so tightly budded on the lovely curve of her large breast. I kissed the other one too, to keep it from being jealous of the attention.

"I didn't ask you to claim me!" She tried to pull away, but I was still balls-deep inside her. She touched the red marks on her clavicle.

The swelling in my cock lessened at that moment and finally I was able to pull out reluctantly from her sweet pussy. A very satisfying gush of my seed followed my actions. It was good to be wolf.

"What? You did, you begged me for it! Come, love, let's bathe together. We have less than forty-eight hours to solve the case before my clan descends on Vegas."

Now she looked confused. And so damn beautiful, her hair wild, her lips red from my kisses. I wanted her all over again, but the need to keep her safe and protected rose. I had to solve the crime, now.

"I...I think I'd better not say anything more. I'm too angry that you just bit me."

"How else was I supposed to claim you? That's the normal way of things." Now she was confusing me. "And I did ask and you said yes. Remember?'

She blushed deep red. "I don't remember anything. Damn it, what does this all mean?"

"You know your history, right? You must know what this means, love. We're Forever Mates. A chosen pair."

Her eyes widened. "But…but I didn't realize what I was saying yes to."

"The deed's done. No going back. We have our whole lives ahead of us. A claiming keeps everyone out of our way, paves the path to eternity for us, my love."

She turned pale. "And if you're wrong, and we're not Forever Mates, then I will never forgive you if I can't shift!"

Esme went paler still and turned and raced away, slamming the suite door behind her.

What the hell? We had just experienced the highest level any wolf or she-wolf could want or aspire to, and she was going to be like that about it? It made no sense. Of course now she would be able to shift — at least, she should be able at some point.

And here I was thinking to marry her when the clan came to town. The Creig would be in her element, helping with the nuptials.

And now this happens?

Chapter Sixteen

Esme

Of all the underhanded, unqualified, despicable things to pull! I took a deep breath, counting to ten before letting it out, ignoring the fact I was standing there stark naked, Lachlan's scent all over my body. Okay, the sex was off the charts, insane even, but to *claim me, mark me, bind me* — all that old shit before we were dead certain that we were absolutely without one iota of doubt remaining meant to be Forever Mates? That was...was... Damn it, I had no proper word for it.

And if he was wrong, then I would lose my biggest dream after finding my Forever Mate — becoming a wolf for real. I'd yearned for that all my life, feeling bad enough about it that I was almost estranged from my family.

Goddamn it all to hell! I wanted to be a wolf more than anything. Well, not more than having the awesome great sex extravaganza I'd been part of all night long, but it was in my top three things to have in my life. The third was to be closer to my family, on an equal basis, not feel like an outsider.

Phttt. Best get cleaned up and make a new plan.

The warm water felt so good, cleansing away all the lusty fragrance of the night before. Surprisingly, I wasn't tired, more energized than anything. I touched the small wound on my shoulder and shook my head. The nerve of that man. Well, he'd pay for that. Just try getting me into bed before I knew the outcome of the bite. *Not going to happen.* He'd have blue balls in no time, and what lovely big balls they were.

Hmm, would I be similarly affected? I did indeed have amazing will power, Lachlan aside. But would it be enough to give me time to teach him a lesson? Was there any antidote for the incessant urge for sex that overcame shifters at times? I ignored the fact that it was considered a precursor of a Forever Mate connection, instead focusing on what I could do to salvage the situation. Maybe my cousin, Dante, the awesome family scientist, would know if there was something I could take to ensure I kept the upper hand?

I dried off quickly, found clean underwear someone had thoughtfully placed in the room, donned one of the dresses that Lachlan had chosen for me, made a face in the mirror and clicked on Dante's phone number to ask him.

"Sorry, Esme, but such a thing does not exist. If you're in that high level of estrus, you're doomed to be in a state of high arousal for some time, I'm afraid."

"Shoot. I'd hoped for better news than that."

"What's going on? Anything the House of Luceres should be warned about?"

Damn it, now I was bringing unwanted attention to myself. I preferred to fly under the radar with my family.

"No, nothing, just wondering for a friend."

Dante was silent for a moment as if he was wondering about the truth of my statement. "Anything else going on with you, Esme? You sound different."

I certainly wasn't going to share a word about being a suspect in a murder investigation. The family would be all over me about it. I needed my way clear to beat everyone to the name of the real murderer. Now that would put Mr. Lachlan Creig of the Highland Heathens Clan in his place.

"I'm good. Just busy with business. It never ends. Too many hauntings, too few ghosts," I joked.

"True. Well, I've got an experiment to get back to."

"Catch you later." I pushed End on my phone and stood still, clicking my fingernail on my front tooth, thinking of my next steps.

I needed to head down to the lobby first, check on the two spinster ladies who were staying in the hotel and have a lovely chat with them and figure out what they knew. *Heck of a coincidence them staying here at the same hotel as the man that was just murdered.*

And it would get my mind off my throbbing pussy. Was it from being used so well or from being horny all over again? I couldn't be certain. I gritted my teeth. *You got this, Esme. Nothing to see here. Spray on lots of perfume and go.*

Not quite as confident as my inner ego insisted I should be, I headed to the door in a cloud of scent and took the hallway that led to the stairwell. *Better to work off some excess energy than chance meeting him in the elevator.* The farther apart we were, the safer my libido and pussy would be.

Sweet goddess. Was that Lachlan striding from the elevator into the lobby? Who else walked the earth like he owned it? *Too freakin' attractive for his own good.* I ducked down behind a large planter filled with green foliage, determined to avoid him at all costs. I was a natural sleuth so I'd gotten used to such actions, always needing to check on people when they least expect it. Then I would know what to do.

Another man must have come up to talk with him as I heard Lachlan greeting him by name.

"Alistair, excellent job on stocking my suite. You deserve a raise, my good man," Lachlan said.

Who the heck was Alistair?

"My pleasure, sire. I am pleased everything was to your liking. Did the young lady find everything to her liking as well?"

So that was the clean underwear guy. What was he to Lachlan and what was with the respectful *sire*? The Vegas gig must pay a lot of money or the casino provided him with someone to take care of his needs. No way could he afford such an indulgence otherwise. His family owned a bed & breakfast, not a castle!

"What is the plan for today, sire? Anything you need?"

"Twenty-five members of my family are arriving tomorrow and I need to make sure all their needs are met. The Creig is especially important to me. I want to ensure that she be treated like the queen she is."

"Your wish is my command. I'll gather the crew and see it done directly."

Crew? How many exactly are in his crew? Had he been lying to me all along? Was he richer than he let on? He did have awfully good, expensive taste in liquor and he'd gotten the penthouse suite without breaking a sweat, jumping the no-dogs policy easily enough.

My right leg was beginning to cramp as I huddled there and I rubbed my calf to ease the pain.

"My oh my, what are you doing hiding down there, dear?" an elderly woman asked, stopping to peer at me over her bifocals. Nice, one of the tour ladies I needed to speak with.

"Just easing a cramp," I said in a low voice, praying that Lachlan hadn't heard me.

"Anything I can do to help?" she asked a bit too loudly for my liking.

With no choice but to stand up, I eased myself to my feet, afraid to look in Lachlan's direction. *If I don't see him, he doesn't exist, right?*

"No, I'm fine now. Miss…?"

"Alice Swenson, and you are our tour guide, Esme Luceres, from last night. One of the people the police suspect of murdering that adulterer. Can't say I blame you. The man is a shameful beast, carrying on like that with a chit of a girl. My goodness, that is some dress." Alice pursed her lips. "I much preferred the long black one. Much more becoming of a lady."

I blushed, surprised she recognized me so easily in the wig. I should have added big sunglasses. "Not my usual choice, but I'm afraid I had to borrow a friend's this morning."

Her eyebrows rose at my indiscretion. "Whatever, dear. How are you doing? Are the police threatening to arrest you yet? Maybe you should go on the lam?"

"But I haven't done anything wrong," I protested.

"That's not what the police think, dear."

I ignored the dig and got right to the point. "Would you have a few moments for a cup of tea or coffee? There's something I would like to ask you, Alice."

She was about to answer when another voice interrupted.

"Esme, I was just looking for you."

No freakin' way. I stayed glued to the spot as Lachlan came into full view. Alice looked from me and back to Lachlan, her eyes wide with interest. Her sister chose that moment to arrive, her expression mirroring Alice's.

"About that tea or coffee?" I hinted, smiling as friendly as I could muster with Lachlan's shadow looming over me. Being so close to him was wreaking havoc on my underwear. *Go away, wolf.* I tried telegraphing the words out of my mind as loudly as possible, hoping he'd get the message.

"Yes, ladies, would you like to join us for breakfast? My treat," he asked.

They tittered together, bestowing admiring looks Lachlan's way, making me look at them with surprise. They were old enough to be his grandmother. And they were chastising *me* about the length of my skirt.

"We'd be delighted," Alice said. "This is my sister June. Our twin nieces will be joining us...will that be all right?"

"Of course. Include them in my invitation as well," Lachlan said.

"Such a gentleman, sister," Alice said.

"Shall we?" he said, indicating the white venetian doors that led to the Garden Café.

Alice and June took off at a fair clip and I had no choice but to trail behind the most annoying wolf in the world. I swallowed my chagrin and pulled the front of my dress away from my neck. They needed to kick up the air conditioning, though the sisters wore cardigans.

Just as we were seated at a table for six, a pair of identical gorgeous dark-haired twenty-somethings dashed into the room. They hurried over to join us, their blue eyes popping at the sight of Lachlan. He got up and helped them to their seats. Somehow, they managed to get between him and me in the seating arrangement. What did I care? They could both have him if all three agreed. Damn it, I did care, a little. If only he hadn't bitten me, we'd still probably been up in the suite, having at it. I fanned myself with the menu.

"Warm, dear?" Alice asked.

"I'm fine."

The waitress came over and eons later, everyone had ordered.

"Now tell us, Lachlan, what's it like to hypnotize a woman?" Twin number one asked, batting her extra-long eyelashes at him, laying one perfectly manicured hand daintily on his forearm. The necklace around her neck caught my attention as it swung forward when she leaned in toward Lachlan, revealing even more cleavage.

Instantly, my legendary temper surfaced. I clenched my teeth, willing myself to stay calm.

"I can tell you what it's like," I said smooth as silk. "Annoying as hell."

Both twins' eyes widened. One asked. "Why annoying?"

"He'll make you look foolish. Dance with you and hand you flowers."

"That would be sweet. I'd like that a lot." Twin number two, who also wore an identical necklace with the same filigree rose charm, gave me a skeptical look before turning all her focus back on the big brawny highlander that didn't seem to be pushing either of them away. Did he need to be so charming? But at least I had learned something of import.

A big-screen TV was turned on in the corner and I glanced over at it to take my mind off things. The news was coming on and I sat up a little straighter. Sara Hatfield, the grieving widow, was on screen, a tissue pressed to her eyes. I went on high alert, not wanting to miss a word the woman had to say.

"Thank you for your condolences. It's been a terrible time. My husband, Danny, was a wonderful man and great father, loyal to a fault until we hired a woman to investigate a so-called haunting at our hotel." She sniffed, her eyes filled with a calculated fury. "A younger woman who could have any man she chose, and now this—he's dead. I told him we should have paid her, even though we weren't happy with her work. She couldn't even find our ghost. Some Ghoststompers." The last part was said with extreme prejudice.

My heart stopped. Sara Hatfield had just singlehandedly destroyed my business and tarnished my good name. In no time, everyone involved would know she meant me. I stumbled to my feet, needing to get away, escape the scrutiny.

"Excuse me," I muttered, then raced away, leaving a number of astonished faces in my wake.

Chapter Seventeen

Lachlan

What had happened? With all these women speaking over one another, I had missed something of vital importance. It was inexcusable that I had let my head be turned by all the attention. I had thought to maybe make Esme a bit jealous, not have her run away in dismay. From me. The thought struck me to the core. I had to act fast.

"If you will excuse me, ladies, I need to check on Esme. Please enjoy your meal." I leaped to my feet and raced after my soul mate. She needed me. Never would I not answer that call. I'd sooner cut off my right arm.

I followed her scent trail to the lobby and out onto the street, hurrying along the sidewalk in quick pursuit. I wanted to shift to wolf, but in town the risks were too great. *Calm down, Lachlan.* Where would she be going? Not to her family, which I would prefer to any other choice—at least they'd keep her safe, hidden from the world until the murder was solved. Because this time, when I caught up with her, I was locking her up in my damn castle, no questions asked.

The lass was fleet of foot, I'd give her that. I tracked her wonderous fragrance many blocks before catching sight of her blue dress and long red wig. *Ah.* I had her now. I doubled my speed, then tripled it, ignoring the odd looks of passersby, intent on reaching Esme and talking some damn sense into her. She should not be out unescorted on the Strip. Exposed—my God, anything could happen! And if one man looked at her the wrong way, so help me. I would turn into a ferocious beast.

I was nearly on top of her now, my feet pounding the pavement in a blur of movement. My body was a well-oiled machine, pumping blood and adrenaline through every vein and artery. I would have enjoyed the chase if not for the worry. Soon I hoped we'd be running through the moors and forests of the Highlands, side by side, with all the excitement and joy such an experience brought.

When I reached her, I swept her up into my arms and kept on running. My duty to my Esme was clear. I would bear her to safety first, find out the facts and adjust the plan accordingly.

"Put me down!" she screamed in my ear, pounding her tiny fists on my back. I ignored her. This precious, dainty, beautiful woman was never getting out of my sight. Ever. Again.

"Hush, love, you don't want the town to think anything's amiss," I cautioned. Not that it mattered. I wasn't stopping for anyone or anything. We were nearly at the casino where I was headlining now and that would be my first stop. A place to get our bearings.

Then order the plane to be made ready and whisk her off to Castle Creigbourne. Someone else could take my place in the show. My magic act that I had spent years on seemed insignificant to me now. A momentary thought of my own clan reminded me I needed to call them and cancel their trip. They needed to stay there for Esme.

"Put me down, Lachlan, I'm warning you! Now!"

Ignoring her, I turned and hurried to the entrance of the hotel on the side of the building that led to my dressing rooms. I wrenched the door open and carted Esme into the theater. The air conditioning welcome after the heated run. When I reached my private suite, I hauled her sweet ass inside and locked the door before setting her down, keeping a close grip on her.

"What the hell! What are you doing? You can't just grab a woman and take her wherever you want. It's more than a little illegal."

"Let's talk about what's bothering you. The Creig always advised good communication in a Forever Mating. It's vital that we start out on a sound footing, love."

"Of all the overbearing, egotistical, patronizing, maniacal, annoying, domineering, insane acts—"

"You forgot arrogant and cocky." I winked at her, trying to charm the lass out of her panties. She looked so gorgeous with her eyes sparking fire and her ample breasts rising and falling under the sundress. I loved every curve. We had time for a mating before I made my calls. Maybe it would calm her, help her to gain perspective. I know it would help me tremendously.

She glared at me, crossing her arms over her chest which only drew my attention all the more.

"What made you run, Esme?"

My question took her aback and she pressed her lips together and shook her head. Now she had me worried. How could I help her if she wouldn't tell me what was the matter?

"Please, *mo ghràdh* — my love, I only want to help." I had never said *please* to a woman before and I nearly stumbled over the word. But it did the trick because she let out a deep breath and I knew she was about to explain. The truth was in her eyes.

"The news was on and Sara Hatfield, the widow of Danny McCoy, was blaming me for his death. She mentioned my company and all, by name." Tears filled her eyes and they were my undoing.

I gathered her into my arms and hugged her tight. "Please don't cry, love. I'm sorry that you're going through this trial. I will fix this. I promise you."

"No one can fix this. Once someone throws slanderous accusations at a person, that's all the public remembers." But her tears lessened as she listened to me.

"*I will fix this.* Once the true murderer is known, they will forget all about it. I don't care what it takes, I'm here for you. We'll hire a marketing team if that's what it takes. Make you out to be a heroine, stage something if we have to. You'll be a shining star in Vegas in no time and everyone will flock to do business with Ghoststompers."

She sniffed, her tears drying up. She pulled away a little. "What will that cost me? So far, I have a bill for an expensive team of lawyers, a private detective crew and now this."

"Let me worry about it. What is money except to be spent on what matters? If you want, you can work off the debt. Be my personal assistant for the rest of your life. Would that sweeten the deal?" I teased, hoping for a smile.

"Hardly!" She swatted my arm. Good, now maybe she'd see reason.

"I want to send you to my home in Scotland... now...before any more unexpected developments. Keep you safe."

"No way! A Luceres does not run from trouble. *Never*. I will work on this case as hard as the next person. Maybe harder. I've got the most at stake."

"You need to be reasonable." I didn't want to tie her up on my bed, but she was pressing the issue too hard.

"You will be seeing more than reason if you don't halt this idea right in its tracks. I'm staying here. That's my final word on it." The glint in her eyes was convincing. She was a worthy mate, my respect doubling in that moment, frustrating as it all was.

"No, I cannot let you do that." I hardened my stance, my words colder. A she-wolf must bend to her mate's wishes. That was what I'd been taught.

"You cannot let me do that! Are you even listening to yourself? This is the twenty-first century, Mr. Lachlan Creig, not eighth century shite. A female chooses for herself now, if you hadn't noticed. And biting me, without my permission, is unforgivable."

"You did agree, you just don't remember it. I would never do it otherwise."

"We'll have to agree to disagree on that. But now, I need to be going. I have a list of things a mile long to do today." She went to step around me and I growled low in my chest, a fearful sound of strongest warning. My wolf rose, ready to assist with the take down.

She froze.

"I can't allow you out of my sight, unless you go to my family. Or your own. It is how it is, love."

"Don't call me that. You don't know if you love me or not. It's way too soon, wolf." And still she defied me.

"You are my Forever Mate — of course I will love you, protect you and keep you happy. It's what an alpha signs up for at birth."

"Signs up for! This conversation is going nowhere. I'm done." She made a gesture with her hands of wiping dust off her palms.

"You will never be done with me now. The die has been cast. If you leave this room, I will chase you to the ends of the earth and back. *Never*, will I let you go. Deal with it."

She swallowed, recognizing the threat to be as real as it got. I could literally see the wheels turning in that pretty little head of hers. Sure, I'm sexist, but that's my programming. What must be done *is* done. Honor to family above all.

"Okay, I can see a compromise is maybe in order. How about I stay in town and we work together? No way am I heading to Scotland."

I considered my words, giving a moment to savor the victory of a proper compromise. "That's more like it, love. Together we'll make an invincible team."

"Rule number one. No more calling me love or any other term of endearment, you seem to have enough of them. Call me Esme or nothing at all. I want to be taken seriously, is that clear?"

My wolf was ready to howl at the moon in frustration at all this compromising, ready to head out and nab the bad guys by the throat. *Lay the prize down at the feet of my queen.*

"As you wish," I said, taking her hand and kissing the palm. I watched her swallow hard, her body trembling with desire. *Let's see how long you can hold off jumping my bones. Then you won't be having a care for whatever I call you, too busy riding the passion and lust of a Forever Mating.*

Chapter Eighteen

Esme

I took a deep breath, praying that my voice would hold steady. Whether I would admit it or not, when Lachlan was riled, he was a tad scary to behold. Maybe even a little more than a tad. *Okay, no need to anger an alpha wolf.* "Now that we have an understanding, have you learned anything else from the detectives about any of the suspects? Anything that can help rule out anyone else?" I kept my own intel back for a moment.

"I was about to call again when you made me chase you through the streets."

"Made you? You didn't have to give chase, wolf."

"It's what we do. Instinct. Alphas cannot stop themselves." He shrugged it off. "Okay, we've found the connection between the elderly sisters and the widow. Turns out Sara Hatfield's daughter, Josie, and their twin nieces Arya and Ava...their only brother's children, are friends. Doesn't look like either of them had anything to do with the case. Just in town visiting."

"That I already knew."

"How could you know that?" he demanded, his expression turning suspicious.

"The necklace. Both twins were wearing the same necklace that Josie was wearing when I spent time in the hotel. When I complimented her on it, she proudly announced she had designed it for herself and only a few existed. A limited edition and one of her signature pieces. They had to be friends or cousins."

"Very clever, Monsieur Hercule Poirot. Are you channeling Agatha Christie now, lass?"

I ignored his already going off script by calling me only Esme, and instead savored the satisfaction of being right for a brief moment, before getting back on the case. But I had to admit, I enjoyed it, pulling one over on Lachlan.

"That leaves the three male suspects, the wife and fiancée," I said, ticking them off on my fingers. "That means we can check out of the suite at the hotel now." Thank goodness, the torture and temptation of knowing *he* was sleeping next door was over. I needed my own space to work through this conundrum. To gain some breathing room, grateful I now had the perfect excuse to abandon the penthouse. Maybe mixed with the *tiniest* bit of regret. I mean, the wolf was an amazing lover. If only he hadn't done what he did. But he was right, no going back on that reality.

"I'm moving us to an undisclosed location until this is over. I've also made arrangements to take a day or two off and have another illusionist step into the breach."

"*What?* I can take care of myself. I'll hole up with a friend. I do have some." I shook my head. No way was I letting him run the show.

My cell rang. I answered it, turning away from the imposing man and diverting my eyes to my phone. Because if I wasn't careful, he'd pull some more voodoo magic and I'd end up doing the bloody tango all the way to an 'undisclosed location'. Whether I liked it or not, I already knew he was more than capable of that feat.

The number on the screen belonged to my friend and business partner, Meghan Hilton, the real gorgeous redhead and not someone wearing a damn wig which was beginning to itch something fierce. Damn, if only I could turn the clock back twenty-four hours and cancel that doomed tour.

"Esme! Are you okay? I just heard on TV that you're in some kind of trouble. Talk to me! What's going on? Why the slam on our business? And what the hell happened at the museum? Somebody was murdered, for heaven's sake!"

"Calm down, Meghan. I'm on top of this. It's not as bad as it looks." Out of the corner of my eye, I noted Lachlan moving away and speaking into his own phone. I needed to make a quick exit, very, very carefully, before he noticed. But how? "I'll explain it all to you later. Don't worry, it's being handled. Top private investigators are on it."

"How can we afford that? That will bankrupt us. Oops, sorry, I mean I know proving yourself innocent is important, but how are you going to pay for it? Did you go to your family? We don't even have enough in checking to cover an expensive team of investigators' daily expenditures."

"It's being taken care of. It won't cost the business anything." Because I would pay back the wolf personally, every damn cent this cost, if I had to moonlight at three jobs.

"What do you want me to do?"

"Just keep everyone calm. This will be over in a jiff." I prayed that my confidence was warranted.

"Please, check in with me lots. I'm worried as hell about you, Esme."

The concern coming through loud and clear in my best friend's voice made me pause. I closed my eyes. She was right. This was a nightmare. What if I couldn't find out the real murderer? Heaven forbid, what if I was arrested for the crime? Lachlan had mentioned that innocents were locked away all the time.

"There's something else I hesitate to mention, but you need to know. Your cousin Cristaldo Luceres called a few minutes ago to speak with you. He sounded pretty pissed on the phone. He said you weren't picking up on your cell."

"What did you tell him?" A new worry popped into my mind, more than having not picked up Cristaldo's call, though in my defense, I'd been a little preoccupied. What would the House of Luceres do if I was the one to drag their name through the mud? That would be worse than the police coming after me. The Tribunal would have my head if I brought dishonor to the Luceres name. *Alphas and their honor, such old-world posturing and as true today as in ancient times. Will they never learn?* But I had to admit a part of me admired their stalwart belief in kith and kin. They were always there for one another. Something I wished I was more a part of at times. But this current situation, this would just ostracize me even more.

"I covered for you. Told him you were busy investigating a haunting and couldn't be disturbed. He told me to have you call him. ASAP."

"Thanks, Meghan." My friend hated lying, so she must have been pushed right up against the wall by Cristaldo. No surprise there, the uber-alpha wolf was the patriarch of the House of Luceres. I glanced over at Lachlan. Hmm, Cristaldo would meet his match in the Highland wolf. I could only imagine the clash of such warriors if they ended up butting heads. *No.* I shook my head. I didn't want that, having either of them hurt defending my honor. Real macho wolf shit still existed in the twenty-first century, unfortunately. No, this would be cleared up long before it came to that. It just had to be.

We said our goodbyes and I dropped the phone back into the pocket of my sundress. Okay. Now what? The only thing I knew for certain was that I would have to lie low, because if one of the Luceres caught sight of me, all hell would break loose. And much as I hated that Lachlan had bitten me, I didn't want to see him hurt. Not when maybe it had been just the tiniest little bit my fault. I had been all over him, craving his touch. Some ancient instinct had cut in, just like two wolves going at it on the battlefield over someone's honor or mate.

Crap. Why couldn't I just shift to wolf and run away, hide in the desert until this thing blew over? The heat of the sun-warmed sand beneath my paws as I loped through the dunes, the tickle of green grass near a thirst-quenching stream, the scent of flowers heightened by dew at night, howling at the full moon, hearing the answering song of other wolves, playing tag with my mate…

What? Stay in the present, Esme. The reality was that possibility most likely ended with Lachlan's bite.

I looked over to see the wolf in question staring at me, his eyes widened by interest.

"Did you see what you just did, love?"

"No, I was a tad too busy worrying about the situation and calming down my best friend and business partner, Meghan. And now that the House of Luceres is on my trail."

"The Luceres know." He pursed his lips. "All the more reason to get you to a safe and secure location right now."

I hated that he was right, though every bone in my body wanted to protest. Soon as I could, I'd find another way to hide out, but with the Luceres in the know, my options were severely limited and the outside world was crashing in fast. They had the resources to unleash hell on me and throw away the key. That was if the cops didn't arrest me first.

"I'll pay you back whatever it costs. Just add it to my bill."

"Alistair is taking care of everything. We just have to slip out the side door to where my limo is waiting for us."

"I hope your credit card can handle all these extra expenses."

"No problem there at all."

I squinted at him, scratching at my hairline where the wig was digging in something fierce. At least in hiding I could throw the damn thing away. "You're awfully cavalier about money."

He reached up and tugged off the offending wig, tossing it onto a counter. My hair fell free around my shoulders and flowed down my back, a heavenly sensation. I ran my hands through it and enjoyed the sensation of the long strands sliding through my fingers.

I didn't like the way he stepped toward me at that precise second, like he was ready for round two. I swallowed, my pussy clenching with sudden urgent need. *No.* Not this again. My fingers fairly itched to grab him now, feel his silky hair, his broad chest pressing against my breasts. My lips parted with the memory. Something shifted behind his eyes, green sparks of light turning to green-fire that entranced. *Promised.*

I had to get out of there! I forced myself to push past the wolf and, with him hot on my heels, so hot with his breath tingling the sensitive skin on my cheek, we headed for the alley. And hoped for freedom.

Chapter Nineteen

Lachlan

I raced down the hallway, Esme at my side. The lass was tormenting me. Her scent. Her beauty. Her intellectual brilliance demonstrated with her great attention to detail, the necklace being a case in point. Oh, but the graceful way she moved, each gesture and nuance a fascination I could study in the tiniest detail for days on end. Even her constantly taking me to task called to me on an elemental level. She had no idea of her power. Her hold on me. I would raze the earth to keep her safe. I had a new plan all right. One that would worry any female in my clan if they knew. But I could trust my brothers to understand.

I'd invited my entire family to stay with us at the mansion Alistair had acquired — more than enough space. And with it purchased by a shell company, no one, let alone the police, would be the wiser about who was living there.

We were almost to the waiting limo when I caught sight of the two annoying detectives. The last thing we needed was to be stopped by those two dweebs. *Why the fuck can't they spend more time on the real suspects and leave my mate the hell alone?* I hustled Esme onto the street, and right into the Mercedes with not a split second to spare.

I decided not to mention their presence to Esme or the look on their faces when they spotted me too late to do anything about it. *Best to spare her the turmoil.* I settled in next to her for the short trip into the desert to our new home.

The detectives I'd hired needed to step up their game. I didn't care if they had to bring in a thousand extra men—I wanted results. And if that didn't work, I'd haul in the remaining suspects and start removing body parts until I had answers.

I took out my phone and texted in my orders. This needed to be over. Now. I had a mate to woo and win, and wanted the space to do it. Though with the number of Creigs about to descend on Vegas, I had better hurry it up. Once my family got wind of the situation, they'd be arranging our lives for us in no time. We'd be handfasted before the day was over. Not that I'd let them interfere with my mate, but the distraction would be there. No extra pressure on Esme would be tolerated.

"Where are we headed?" Esme asked, looking pensive.

"Not far. Just a few miles. I thought it best to stay close to town to keep an eye on things." And more importantly to the airport in case I had to squire her away at a moment's notice to Castle Creigbourne. I was having a helipad built at the newly acquired mansion, but that would take time before it would be completed, and a helicopter delivered. A runway would also be built of course, one that would allow easy coming and going of one of our Learjets. A permanent Vegas home was important now that the Creig clan and the House of Luceres would become family.

The limo turned into the long driveway, soon revealing our newly acquired home. Hmm, was it fine enough, spacious enough, grand enough for my queen? It was imposing with its Italian Renaissance-style, and the seventy room home big enough for my family did feature marble imported from Italy and Africa, much like the Vanderbilt home built on Rhode Island back in the day.

But would Esme like it? I'd chosen it for the intimate connection to Italy, where her family came from originally, hoping she would appreciate the sentiment. Somehow, I had to charm the panties off her again. I'd paid the owners triple what the mansion was worth if they'd vacate within the hour. A team of experts were now going over the house with a fine-tooth comb to make certain it was up to my standards.

"We're staying at the famous Breakers Mansion? Like the one on Rhode Island? How on earth did you manage that? No freakin' way a credit card can manage this feat. What's going on here, and tell me the truth, or so help me goddess I'm out of here!"

How else to protect her if not with my money and brawn? Now she sat staring at me with accusing eyes. Such beautiful eyes too. Full of wonderous blue light, when she wasn't pissed at me for something like right now.

"I had to do something to keep you safe. And my family expects decent accommodations when they arrive tomorrow. I'll not have them living second class."

"Decent! The Super Ten on the outskirts of Vegas is decent…the YMCA is decent…this is way over the top! Crap, it has a tennis court, bowling alley, full-sized theater, ballroom and two…*two* swimming pools. What kind of family needs all that?"

I stiffened. "I'll not have my family spurned. They deserve the best much as anyone. So I like to indulge a bit. It's not like I didn't earn it fair and square."

She shook her head. "You didn't tell me you were uber-rich. It was all a con, wasn't it? From the beginning, the pretending not to care I'm a Luceres, the bite, then this!"

"I did not con you. I am who I am. I'm no different now from before. Just the same man with ample funds to make this world easier to navigate. Is that so wrong? Wanting to acquire wealth that makes life better? You will benefit too, Esme."

I would never apologize for who or what I stood for. The lass would need to learn that, respect that as I would respect her and how she wanted to live her life. With me in it, of course. That went without saying.

"When this case is solved, I'm *so* out of here. Is that clear enough? I won't be lied to like this. Not by anybody and not by an uber billionaire. That's what you are, right?"

Maybe hiring a staff of fifty to see to our needs might seem a bit much, but I considered it essential for her. And my family. But my pulse rate had increased with the challenge she'd laid down. But I swore by all the alphas that had come before me that by the time I'd hauled the murderer's ass before a judge, she'd have forgotten all about ever thinking to leave me.

"Money is but a means to an end. I spent my life learning how to increase wealth so that I could do the things I want, and one of those things is create magic for an appreciative audience, give them an hour or two with no need to think of anything but the moment. And money enough to aid important charities, but I also want my Forever Mate to live as she should, have the best of things, whatever she needs."

"What I *want* is to figure out who stabbed Danny McCoy with a syringe while taking my tour and get them to confess. I'm ready to throttle it out of them myself!" She shook her head. "And now my family's going to get involved. I can only imagine what the Tribunal is going to do about it."

"The Tribunal?"

"The group that oversees the three houses of Italian wolves in Vegas: Luceres, Anche and Ribelle. They're like the Supreme Court of the United States, only for shifters. Senatores, who run the Curia Court located underground of the Anche Casino, are notorious for wanting to keep the status quo and come down hard on anyone stepping out of line. Drawing unwanted attention to us is a huge no-no. And this FUBAR situation I've fallen in is not going to sit well with them." She chewed on her thumbnail, her worried expression not to my liking.

"They have no say over you now. You're with me. They try one thing, harm one hair on your head, and so help me God, I will not be held accountable for my actions."

She stared at me like I had grown two heads, her eyes widening. "But you don't understand. Their word is law. I'm bound to answer to them."

I shook my head. "No, not anymore. You're a Creig now. We'll be handfasted today if possible. Then they can no longer bother you."

"No way. I'll not be railroaded into anything. Bad enough you bit me!"

That again. My head began to pound, though one thing was clear. She needed to have me look out for her. Every second of every day, no matter what it took, I would protect her.

With my life if necessary.

Chapter Twenty

Esme

The famous Breakers Mansion loomed at the end of the driveway. I had to ask myself, a quick reality check, was Esme of the House of Luceres losing her damn mind? Allowing herself to be walled up in that house? Sure, it was gorgeous, all scrumptious Italian architecture and luxury galore. But to think for one moment that I belonged in such a place... No, I had to keep my head about me. This was only temporary, a day or two at most. I would never allow it to become my prison.

The ridiculously handsome charismatic wolf at my side was going to drive me insane. Why was all this stuff suddenly happening to me? Maybe I needed more than a reality check — a bump upside the head might not go amiss. Because, through all this damn turmoil, all I could think about was jumping his gorgeous bones. His woodsy scent underlaid with musk was driving me to distraction as much as I worked to ignore it. But making love was the last thing I could allow to happen, considering the last go around. I'd been entirely shameless, letting him in like that. *Then he bites me.* I growled at the memory. How dare he?

"Are you okay? You just growled."

"Fine," I said through gritted teeth. *Just keep thinking about that damn bite, that will help. Stop me from acting on my lust.* Did he say I growled? I never growled! I was unable to shift and only real shifters ever growled. Well, that was the least of my problems at the moment.

"Everyone's ready to greet you, Esme. See, they're all lined up in front of our new home."

"It's not *our* home. It's yours, damn it."

His mouth firmed into a straight line. The sudden chill in the air gave me a slight stab of guilt. After all, he was trying to be helpful. We needed each other at the moment, maybe me more than him. I certainly couldn't go home and take the chance of being arrested by the detectives or confronted by Cristaldo Luceres. The realization did not sit well.

But damned if it was going to make me play nice and change the very fabric of my being. I considered myself a decent person, caring about my friends and family. But this guy, this particular wolf, damn it, he brought out something different in me. Something annoying as hell.

"Are you capable of being nice to my employees, Esme?"

The car had pulled up and the mostly smiling line of forty or fifty people looked eager for us to get out of the limo.

"Of course. Why would you question that? I'm a nice person, according to my friends."

"Good. Perhaps you can treat them like friends. I suppose I can't expect the same in return, but fine. Let's do this thing."

Lachlan got out before I could say a single word in rebuttal and stalked toward his employees. He greeted each one in turn, a charming host that easily made every one of them feel comfortable and maybe even a little special in the way he seemed to take a real interest in what they had to say. It was a side of him I hadn't been party to before and I had to admit, I liked it.

I did my best to be agreeable, which wasn't exactly hard or taxing, then trooped into the mansion, catching Lachlan out of the corner of my vision busy talking to a group of his employees. Well, his choices didn't suck, that was for certain. This was like walking into the palace at Versailles. My cell rang, interrupting my trance, and I answered Meghan's call.

"What's up?"

"Code ten emergency! A family needs your help, right now! Their young son was attacked by a ghost or maybe a demon —"

"Text me the address and meet me there. I'm on my way!"

I made a full one-eighty and headed back out to the limo. Clambering inside, I gave the driver directions that Meghan had already texted in. With a code ten there was no time to wait. My heart rate jacked up just at the thought.

I could probably be back before his nibs even noticed I was gone. Or not. But what did it matter? I was my own woman and nobody told me what to do. Nobody.

The driver soon had me back in town and headed straight to the address of the haunted family. Meghan would have the Ghoststompers van that contained all our equipment. When a child was at risk, nothing got in the way.

Of course, Lachlan called my cell.

"No time to talk now. I've got an emergency—a child needs my help. I'm with Meghan. Talk later. And do not, I repeat, do *not* under any circumstances, come here. I'm working and this is my business." I hung up on his protestations then turned my phone off. No distractions allowed.

"Would you like me to wait, miss?"

"No, I'll call an Uber when I'm done. It could be hours and hours." I had no idea what we were facing inside. It could be the real deal or just a child in torment for some reason. Either way, I was going to get to the bottom of it so that the child could be helped. By a therapist if necessary. But if it was a real haunting, a rare occurrence, then I needed to bring my A-game. Leave all my worries behind and prepare myself.

I took a few deep breaths standing on the street in front of the very normal-appearing three-bedroom suburban bungalow. Well, normal other than the fact the door had been left wide open. I centered my thoughts, asking for the strength to withstand whatever force was inside the house. I added an extra entreaty to the universe. *Give me the courage of my convictions, oh goddess, allow me to face whatever happens with resolve.*

"Thank goodness, you're here!" Meghan came flying out of the back of the van, her arms loaded down with equipment. She gestured with a head nod as she scurried toward the sidewalk. "There's more inside."

I climbed into the back of the van and retrieved the final items, then joined her on the front steps.

"I wonder why the door's been left wide open?" she asked.

"Maybe they're thinking to leave an escape route for the entity. Are they still here?" I asked.

"Yes. They said to come on in."

"Okay." That too wasn't normal. But if there was an angry ghost or demon inside, then no one would venture in for long anyway. Hmm, maybe a few more crooks or criminals needed to encounter a demon or two doing their dirty work? It might cut down on incarcerations when a thief was scared silly. Serve them right, too.

"Hello, is anyone home? It's Ghoststompers Inc., your friendly neighborhood ghost chasers," I called, stepping inside. Immediately I felt the extreme chill of the front living room. I didn't need a thermal heat reader to know that it wasn't the air conditioner working overtime, My breath formed into mist in front of my face. The only other thing to cause this kind of cold would be an ice plant out back.

"Looks like we got a live one," Meghan said, her light blue eyes widening until I could see a rim of white around the blue.

Meghan had a love-hate relationship with ghosts, the same as I did. I preferred the ones that were easily nudged along with a gentle reminder. But every once in a long while we'd find one that had been trapped here for centuries, growing stronger, more often than not because a home was built over an ancient burial ground.

"Yes, definitely. You brought the ghost traps?" I asked.

She nodded, sucking in her lower lip. "Uh-huh, a four pack."

The pneumatic ghost traps I'd invented through trial and error were the best way to remove a ghost who refused to exit a residence. I'd installed wire sensors inside the tempered glass devices to detect temperature and electromagnetic frequency. All we had to do was wait until a ghost entered, sending readings to a remote-control device, and *boom*, they were captured inside the device, unable to escape.

The device required a lure much like fishing, usually something that had belonged to the deceased in their lifetime that would arouse their curiosity enough for them to venture inside. I knew they were there when the readout went blank and a blue swirl was seen inside. Nothing could get in once the trap slammed shut, and more importantly, nothing could get out. Then it was just a matter of transporting the jar to a graveyard and releasing them back into the wild.

Suddenly a man and a woman appeared in the doorway, their faces drawn and pale, and both of them wearing layers of warm clothing.

The tired-looking middle-aged man stepped forward, offering his hand. "Thanks for coming. I'm Greg and this is my wife, Nora. Our son Jack's hiding under the dining room table and won't come out. I'm not certain what to do. Should we just pull him out, or what?"

"No. Take me to him. I need to see what surrounds him first," I said. Shivering in my sundress, I wished I had thought to bring a sweater. At least Meghan had pants and long sleeves, far more appropriate for the job. Another thing I could blame the wolf for.

"Meghan, can you get a reading on the EMF meter? Any idea of what we're dealing with would be helpful."

In the dining room, the long wooden table had been covered with a big blanket that draped down to the floor. I caught a faint whiff of something that smelled like it had gone bad. *Par for the course.* Investigating hauntings was not for the faint of heart. It was just the smiles of gratitude when it was all over that kept me going. Well, unless the owner wanted a ghost that didn't exist.

"He insisted on the blanket," Greg said, spreading his hands wide like he had no idea what else he could have done.

"That's fine."

I bent down and lifted the edge of the dark wool blanket slowly, spotting a young boy of around eight years old a few feet away, huddled into a tiny ball, his eyes huge in his thin face. "Hey, Jack, nice fort. I don't want you to be worried about anything. I'm just here to help you. My name is Esme."

He remained silent, but his hands twitched and his eyes widened. He looked frozen to the spot and my heart squeezed in sympathy for his plight. He had no idea what was going on, just that he felt compelled to hide himself away.

"I'm getting a reading here," Meghan said, her voice rising with excitement. "Three separate entities, all hovering just below the table legs. Must be one story down then, in the basement. This is just the end of the portal, not the beginning."

Damn. I hated basements with every fiber of my being. Too many bad things lingered belowground, all of them usually taking an instant dislike to me interfering with their good times.

The table banged up and down, as if confirming Meghan's diagnosis.

Jack whimpered and I'd had enough. These entities were going to be eliminated in short order no matter what it took.

"Okay, that means the traps need to be set down there. Where's the door to your cellar, Greg?" I asked.

"Over there." He pointed to a narrow entrance just off the dining room in the hallway.

"We'll need to light the lanterns and prepare the ghost traps," I said to Meghan. "Do you know anything about the people who lived here before you, Greg?"

"Not really." He shared a look with his wife. "They were long gone before we moved in. The real estate agent only mentioned one name, Vinny Caltrain, I believe. The house had stayed vacant for nearly a year before we bought it. I think I know why now," he added ruefully.

Holy shite, same last name as fedora guy! Was he related to the person who'd been on the tour, Albert Caltrain? Either this was one hell of a coincidence or, more likely, fate and the goddess were pointing something out to me. I worked to gather myself. I had a family to help. There would be time enough to check this all out later.

"Did they leave anything behind? Something you might have found abandoned in one of the cupboards?"

Greg shook his head, but a look passed over Nora's face that said she knew something.

"What is it, Nora? It's best to bait the trap with something that the spirit wants. Did you find anything?"

"Yes, I did." She began to wring her hands. "A shoebox."

Greg looked at his wife in surprise. "You didn't mention a shoebox."

"I didn't want to have to turn it in. I found some money. A lot of fifties and hundreds and I knew you might turn it in. I wanted to keep it for a rainy day."

"Did you spend some of it?" I asked. The ghosts might be angry about losing their stash. Stranger things had happened. Well, wasn't money the root of all evil?

"A little. Just to buy Jack some things he was wanting...you know...to keep up with his friends."

"Is there still some left? Because we'll need to set the ghost traps with some bills to get them to enter. Then we can remove them."

"Will I get it back?"

Greg gave her a look and she blushed bright red. "Sorry, of course, for Jack, anything you need."

"Great. Okay, you get the shoebox and we'll head downstairs to see what we're faced with."

Meghan and I hauled the equipment to the top of the stairs, sharing the weight between us. I tried the light switch, but of course it didn't work.

"Okay, let's light the lantern." It would have been foolhardy to go in with a battery-charged flashlight—ghosts just love to absorb the energy and become stronger.

After carefully lighting a propane lantern with a match, I held it high and began to descend the spooky staircase. Yup, it even had cobwebs and spiders galore, just for atmosphere. I swallowed and was immediately sorry for opening my mouth—the stench would curl someone's hair and it coated the inside of my mouth, making me gag. I braced for whatever awaited us down below, feeling more uneasy with every step.

At the bottom, I peered around the semi-darkness. Right, fairly easy to spot. Three areas that swirled in the darkness, like black holes ripped in the universe, spinning close together. And it was obvious they were angry. I closed my eyes, wishing they would suck each other in over the event horizon that scientists always went on about and vanish completely. I opened my eyes. Nope, no such luck.

Leave.

The word penetrated my skull with considerable force. Yes, I wanted to, but I wanted to help Jack more.

"Let's set up the traps over there on those barrels." I pointed them out to Meghan as she reached the cellar floor.

She nodded, looking pale but calm. "It sure stinks down here."

"No kidding. Let's just get this done."

I slid the first trap from the carry box and carefully laid the apparatus on the flat top of the barrel. When all three were in place, I lit three small candles and placed them toward the back of the thick glass device, leaving room for the cash to be laid just inside the door as enticement. I didn't need the money catching on fire.

"Hello, I have the cash," Nora spoke out, her voice echoing down the staircase. She obviously wasn't coming down so I went back up the stairs to retrieve it.

She handed over a few bills and I thanked her. Trudging back down the twelve steps, I folded a couple of hundreds and laid them in each of the ghost traps in turn. Then Meghan handed me two of the remotes while she held the third. Now we waited and remained silent.

The three dark voids shifted around, one finally breaking away from the pack and drifting over to the barrels. *Yes, just a bit farther. Take a look – see? There's money to be had.* And for once cash turned into a very useful device because inside the glass canister the spirit went. I hit the button on my handheld device, the closing thud a very satisfying sound indeed, and ghost number one was trapped.

I wanted to high five Meghan, but I knew to wait. There were still two to go and anything could happen.

We settled back down to wait, the two dark masses expanding and contracting like the strike of a heavy drumbeat, energy bouncing in time to something otherworldly, something I didn't want to hear. A second spirit began to move carefully and cautiously toward another one of the ghost traps. *Please, just a bit farther...you know you want to.*

I had to wonder about the money. What had it been for? Why did these three tormented spirits feel such a connection to it? Something important that I would try to learn in the days ahead. I liked my final report to a client to be thorough.

The second ghost was getting closer, the candle wavering a bit from the action outside the glass bottle. Then he slipped in and Meghan hit her switch, locking the spirit inside.

Thank goodness. Only one to go. But he or she would be the most cautious now. Maybe so much so that we'd be waiting for hours in hopes that they might venture inside.

Loud footsteps echoing overhead didn't help the situation any. The ghost moved farther away, like they were thinking of departing. *Great.* Who had come into the house and disturbed the entity? I hoped my first guess wasn't right.

Down the stairs the bootsteps continued and I didn't need to turn my head to know who was standing and sucking up all the air in the basement. But of course the entity became more skittish and nearly vanished from view.

I put my forefinger to my mouth and gave Lachlan a stern look, shaking my head. To his credit he remained silent, just hovered in the background. Meghan gave me a look once she took in the giant Scotsman in the kilt standing at the bottom of the stairs. A look that said *wow, what have you been hiding from me, girlfriend?* In reply, I rolled my eyes and shook my head.

My emotions overwhelmed me for a moment, thinking of all the things I wanted to tell the wolf about why he should have stayed away. But now was not the time. Meghan nudged me and gave me an even odder look. I mimed, *what?* At her.

She pointed at her eyes then at me, like she'd seen something. I shrugged, having no idea what she was going on about. The third dark spirit stayed mostly hidden, its energy tighter now. Then slowly it began to inch forward, creeping like the sun moving across the sky. At this rate we'd be stuck here till nightfall and then some. And I really disliked being trapped in with ghosts, especially angry, unhappy ones, after dark.

A bit of a soft glow began behind me. I turned to observe Lachlan with his hands raised, palms up, his mouth moving silently as if in prayer. His eyes were closed and his head upturned to the heavens, as if speaking to someone. I stared, mystified, at the image he created. *Now he's channeling a saint!*

But I could not deny it was working.

The spirit began to move more quickly, but not toward the third ghost trap—toward Lachlan. It hovered in front of him, the mist moving like it had a heartbeat, before it began to lighten and dissolve into nothingness. A slight glimpse of something for a split second made me wonder. Was that for real? I shook my head. No way was I seeing beyond the veil. *Hell, I can't even shift.*

"How can you be certain it's gone?" I whispered at him, filled with outrage. With our luck the ghost was just taking a time out and would be back to haunt the family after we left. I would far prefer to haul its ass out the door in a ghost trap. Then I would know we'd done our job properly. But no denying the 'ghost whisperer' was something to watch.

He gave me a confident look. "The spirit has gone. He just needed to have his say before moving on."

"Well, what was his problem?" I demanded.

"Someone paid to have him killed. Same as the other two. Their remains are buried in the basement."

Shocked to the core, I could only stand there and gape at him. Meghan wasn't faring much better, swiveling her head between Lachlan and me.

"No freakin' way," I finally said when I could find my voice, cognizant of young ears upstairs.

He nodded. "My promise to see justice done helped him to make the decision to move to the light. Now we've got more murderers to solve, but a promise is a promise. And I think I can safely say that there is a possible connection to the current case."

"Right. The former owner of this house was named Vinny Caltrain and could be related to Albert." Every hair on my head electrified as interest zinged through me. "I really like it when the dead can speak up and let the living know they were murdered. Well, unless there was another murderer in the tour group that night? Always possible."

I shuddered and glanced over at the barrels. "Are there bodies in there?" I asked, pointing at them.

"No, all three are buried beneath them. The barrels are just filled with cement to act as a decoy. Makes them too heavy to move. It's an ideal hiding spot because no one could be bothered to have such heavy items taken out."

"And the ghost told you all that?" I asked, mystified and annoyed in equal measure.

"Right. Now I need you to explain something for me."

His face grew stern and his eyes glittered with energy, an energy that rolled off him in waves. And he stood between me and the staircase that promised freedom, a giant among men and wolves.

Chapter Twenty-One

Lachlan

The lass had the grace to look abashed before the look of cocky disregard for her own safety returned. How could my billions save her if she was in such total denial?

"And I need you to step out of my way!"

"Not until you promise to stop all this. I won't have my woman running around putting herself in harm's way."

"*Your* woman!"

"Umm...excuse me, but I'd like to get out of here. I think you both should discuss this alone or another time? We need to finish up and report in to the family. Let them know they're safe again," Meghan said, her tone neutral.

Esme and I stared at each other. The sound of voices overhead sealed the deal.

"Fine. Let's get this over with. But if you think for one second I'm letting this go, think again, Esme."

My Forever Mate said nothing except with her eyes that shot daggers at me. She turned and began to gather up their equipment, carefully sliding the ghost traps into a handy carrier.

"I can see to it that those ghosts are sent on," I said.

"No need. I'll let them loose far from here, in a cemetery where they'll feel right at home."

"Better for their spirits to be sent to the light than left for all eternity with other strange ghosts they don't know," I said.

I heard her take a full breath into her lovely lungs. "*Fine*. But not until later."

"Let me carry that." I took the box without giving her time to argue or make a federal case of it and headed back up the stairs.

"Is it all done then?" the man asked, his arms around his wife and son. The trio looked worn-out but relieved.

"It is." I pointed at Esme who was closely following on my heels. "She'll fill you in."

"All three ghosts are contained. You're safe now."

"Thank God," the man said, sharing a relieved look with his wife. "And thank you." He held out his hand for a shake.

Esme shook it. "Just glad I could help. Getting Jack to come out from under the table is all the thanks I need. There was a lot going on in your basement. I'll write up my report and send it by email. Then you can decide what you want to do."

She was hedging now, wanting to spare the family and give them time to recover before they had to deal with the police. Having the bodies exhumed would be a big deal in its own right.

"Why? What else did you learn?" The husband and father pressed for answers. I understood—a man needed to know everything to keep his family safe. I was totally on his side.

Esme clamped her lips together.

"I think you should tell them, lass."

She blessed me with a murderous look before saying, "Maybe we should all sit down. The information is a bit jarring."

"We need to know. But I think Jack should go to his room, Nora."

"No, Dad. I want to stay and I don't want to be alone. What if they come back?"

"They won't come back," Esme said. "We trapped them, just like you do a mouse with cheese."

"Really?" Jack said, his eyes rounding in wonder. "Can I see?"

I dutifully held out the box of ghost traps and showed the family the proof. Two of the canisters were swirling with energy, a pulsating darkness, proof positive that spirits resided inside.

"They were two ghosts?" the man asked.

"No, three."

"Where's the other one?" he asked, his eyes worried.

"He headed for the light," I said. "Once I promised to catch his murderer."

"The ghost talked to you?" Jack asked. He gave me a look usually reserved for superheroes.

I bent down and looked the small lad in the eyes. "He did. And now he's in heaven with his family."

"Cool. But what about those two?" Jack asked, pointing at the traps. "Do they get to move on too?"

"Yes." I stood and faced the man. "You might want to have the house blessed by a man of God. A priest or minister, or person of faith. That will ensure they can never return."

"But why were they here in the first place?"

"Okay, but I'd like us all to sit down first," Esme said, her quiet tone reassuring.

I hadn't seen much of this side of her. She was usually such a spitfire. But she handled the next few minutes well, explaining what would need to be done now by the family.

When it was over, the family looked paler, but I could see they were resolved to work things out. Once the skeletons were removed, they could stay as long as they wanted. If they wanted. Sometimes a fresh start was best.

"Thanks again," the man said as he showed us out. "I can't speak highly enough of Ghoststompers, Inc. I'll be singing your praises all over social media at once."

"Thanks, we could use the endorsement," she said in a rueful tone of voice.

I could see the man's curiosity was stirred by her words, but he was too tired to deal with any new information at the moment. Probably for the best. Knowing your business consultant was involved with her own murder problems might be a bit unsettling, unfair as it all was. Even under such duress, Esme had come to another's aid.

As angry as I was for putting herself at risk, it did say something about her true character. The words from The Creig about compromising with a mate did strike a chord, but still, I held on to my righteous anger. I couldn't bear the memory of Mary. It still cut me to shreds. Esme would just need to understand, if not now, maybe one day. I would never compromise on safety, no matter how long I lived or how much it annoyed my Forever Mate.

The three of us walked to the curb, and I waited for Esme to say goodbye to her friend and business partner.

"Take as long as you need. I'll wait in the limo."

She laid the canisters in the back of the van with the other equipment and turned on me, hands on hips, nostrils flaring. Meghan closed the door and scurried off to wait in the driver's seat. "I'm going back with Meghan, and that's final!"

"Over my dead body!"

"That can be arranged!"

Angry as she was, all I wanted to do was pick her up and bear her to my castle. I looked around. Was anyone watching? I was about to act when a siren pierced the air. *Oh Lord*, not the police. Was Esme going to be arrested now? I should have told her about them showing up at the casino that second time. No time now to do anything but get her the hell out of there.

I raced toward her but she hustled away into the front seat of the van like she knew what was about to happen, locking the door to keep me out. I pounded on the glass.

"Let me in or so help me —"

She just flipped me the bird before the van took off, leaving me in the lurch.

Esme

"Drive, Meghan," I urged, realizing in the instant I gave Lachlan the finger I was acting about as immature as it gets. Then why did it feel so darn satisfying?

"Guy sure seems to have a thing for you," she commented with a huge smirk on her face. We passed a police car and I recognised the two detectives who had been shadowing me. I ducked down, praying they hadn't seen me.

"Don't go there, okay? I'm under enough pressure without that smug kilt-wearing Neanderthal thinking he can say or do anything he wants."

"The police are gone. You can sit up now. Well, it was obvious the guy's darn good at talking to spirits. Maybe we should hire him? Save on making all those expensive ghost traps. Having that glass apparatus made up for each one-time use is cost prohibitive." She gave me a quick look.

"We would have gotten the third ghost if he hadn't been there. It would just have taken longer. And it's not like we use many traps in a year. So few ghosts, so many 'hauntings'." I air-quoted the word. *Have Lachlan join our team? Never going to happen.* I had escaped that mess if not with my dignity intact, then at least with my resolve alive and functioning.

But where to go? I knew he'd tail me, to the ends of the earth if necessary. That left one place, and I really, really didn't want to go there.

"You seem different, Esme. In the basement, when you were dealing with those ghosts, for a minute there, I swore I saw your eyes flash the brightest blue. What's going on?"

"So much that I don't know where to start." My eyes changing like that was intriguing, though I had no time to dwell on it.

"Well, we got miles to go on this 'catch and release' mission, so start at the beginning."

When I got to the point of the story where Lachlan had bitten me, Meghan gasped, "What? No permission? The *bastard*!"

Surprisingly, I didn't like the word applied to him. He'd been kind of under the sway of the lust goddess as much as me. Maybe more. He was an ancient shifter endowed with the telltale genetic code necessary to procreate the species.

"Well, we were going at it rather hot and heavy." I squirmed in my seat. "I was saying *yes* a lot. We might have gotten our signals crossed."

"Still, it's unforgivable." She shook her head. "No wonder you're in such a tizzy. Now, you may never be able to shift. Well, unless it turns out he is your Forever Mate. Is that possible?"

"He's definitely *not* my Forever Mate. Okay, give it a rest." I wished I felt as confident about it as my words suggested. Then I felt bad for being rude. "Sorry, Meghan, I guess I'm in more of a mess than I realized."

"I forgive you. I get it. Your life is in a state of flux. Oh, here we are."

At that moment I was extra grateful for her sunny disposition, so different from my own skeptical self.

The Oakwood Cemetery loomed before us, the broad gates guarded by a stone angel on each side, their wings reaching for the sky. There was room here for the two ghosts, if they chose to stay on. Most of the other spirits had long since departed, especially back in the oldest part.

"Good. Now we can off-load these souls and wish them well." I realized that Lachlan's limo driver was following us, at a discreet distance. I just hoped he had the good sense to stay inside the vehicle.

"They sure are dark spirits. Rather unusual. But I guess being murdered left them in a deplorable frame of mind." Meghan made a face of understanding.

"And when the family began to spend the money the murderer had left—and I have to wonder how on earth *that* happened—they got really mad. There must be a connection between the money and the murderers. You know, with three murders, that's a serial killer situation."

"Yeah, leaving the money behind is weird. Who does that?"

True. Everyone I knew cared way too much about the all-mighty dollar to leave anything to chance.

When Meghan had parked the vehicle by the curb in the oldest, shadiest part of the graveyard, we both jumped out and headed for the back of the van.

I handed her one of the ghost traps and took up the other. All we needed to do was set the timers so the spirits didn't get out too soon. I wanted to be a long way away before they exited the devices. All I needed was one of those suckers clinging onto me for a lift home! That was how the urgent requirement for an immediate exorcism could be created. And that was not a pretty sight.

Out of the corner of my eye I spotted a blur of movement. *No. Not now.* I sent the words forcefully from my mind to see if Lachlan could catch them. Because if it was remotely possible we were Forever Mates, he should be able to read me telepathically. Especially since he had the gift of second sight. If not, I rested my case.

"All set?" I asked, watching Meghan fidget with the device to set the timer switch.

"Yeah, I think so. I set it for twenty minutes. It was acting weird. The spirit inside may have been causing the issue, but it should be fine now."

We both carefully set the ghost traps down between two graves that had never contained any ghosts and backed up. Seemed there were a few more ghosts hovering around the graveyard this evening than usual, shadowy people that couldn't leave this realm for the hereafter for some reason. A sense of profound sadness filled me. I shook it off and turned to Meghan.

"Time to get out of Dodge, girlfriend." We high-fived this time and made a beeline for the van.

My phone buzzed with a text just as Lachlan appeared, standing right in my path. I frowned and pulled out my cell and read the text from my co-worker Nancy Fields at the museum.

The police are here and are going through your locker. What do you want me to do?

Shocked at the idea of the invasion of my personal property, I stumbled. Lachlan grabbed my arm to prop me upright. Him being so close, though comforting on one level, made my lady parts far too happy. I gritted my teeth, wishing the shifter life came with a damn manual. Or at least an antidote for this extreme level of lust. I mean, if no one else had been present, I would have been rolling on the grass with him behind the nearest tombstone. And ghosts be damned.

"What is it, Esme?"

"The police are searching my locker at work."

Meghan gasped. "What the heck! Why would they do that? Crap, are they going to arrest you, Esme?" she asked, her face ashen.

"No, they are not," Lachlan said with such confidence I instantly felt better. "I'm taking you back to my place to keep you safe. Now that we know who the murderer most likely is, I'm having my team find him, follow and investigate him. They will acquire all the evidence needed to send him to prison for the rest of his days."

"I guess that was a tie," I said, relieved my voice was less shaky. I hated sounding weak because I wasn't.

"We both discovered the murderer together." Now I just had to hope that the team of lawyers and investigators got their act together quick enough to get the heat off me. Why did those two detectives have the hots for me? Was it the Luceres name? Did they want the good press that comes from taking down a so-called rich celebrity to pad their resume and look good to their fellow officers?

"Ah, guys, I think we'd better be getting out of here. The ghost traps are going to spring open soon," Meghan advised, glancing back nervously at the two glass canisters lying on the ground.

Another text alert.

They found something in your locker. A vial of liquid. They look happy about it.

I groaned and read off the text.

Meghan's eyebrows rose. "What the heck is that about?"

"It's not mine. Somebody must have planted it. Which means somebody's trying to frame me."

Lachlan growled.

I distantly heard the sound through the heat of anger that coursed through my brain. *How dare they!* If I got my hands on the person who was trying to set me up, so help me goddess, I'd tear them limb from limb. My body felt electrified, like it was ready to throw off its own skin. It was such an odd sensation I was taken aback. And to think about tearing someone apart at the seams…not exactly my usual MO. What was going on with me? I shook my head, trying to make sense of it all.

The two of them were staring at me now, as if I'd grown two heads.

"What?"

"Nothing. We'd better get a move on," Meghan said. She hurried to get into the van, slamming the door shut.

Chapter Twenty-Two

Lachlan

I was prepared to cart Esme kicking and screaming back to the limo. It was for her own good, after all. But first, I'd try common sense, something that I've found all too often *not* to be that common in the supernatural world.

"You need to be somewhere safe for the next day or two, until this matter is settled."

"You think I don't know that? I've got the cops on my tail, some unknown person trying to frame me for murder and you doing your level best to drive me crazy."

"Is that all? I would think that as someone who advertises herself as a Ghoststomper, that would all be in a day's work."

At least she looked less stressed now, trying to hide a small smile.

"And you got less than a minute to decide. The canister is going to pop open in the next twenty seconds. I'd rather not be taking an extra passenger back to our place. Those two spirits are not ready to move on. Not until their murderer is found."

She frowned, like she was not happy with what she was going to say. "Our place, is it? Okay, but only if you keep your distance. I want my own wing, far away from yours. Understood?"

"Understood." I hid a smile. Right, like I had to worry about that. Soon as I had her safely back under my roof, I'd up my game. Esme was the one for me. Running away to help a family and a small child in need, that only made her an even more rare gem in my opinion. Much as I hated her putting herself at risk, she'd done a good job trapping those two ghosts. And she was in one piece. To think of what might have happened to her, I just couldn't go there.

POP.

POP.

"Run! Get in the limo!" I shouted. The two dark spirits were already moving across the ground at the lightning speed as only the unearthly can manage, gaining on us.

No time left. I had to act. Now. In a blur of light and movement, I stripped and shifted to wolf, standing in front of Esme to protect her from the dark cloud of anger.

I stiffened my back legs, snarling at the swirling black mass. The angry spirits tried to move around me, their intention clear. Catch a ride on the lovely soul who didn't have the sense to get inside the damn limo, but just hovered behind me, gasping.

One dark soul slipped away from the other, focused on getting past me, eager to get at her. I had no choice now. I clawed at the seething life force with my massive front paws, breaking it up, damaging its ability to reform.

The second *ka* came at me then, its strength far fiercer than the first. In life the person had been already damaged, a dead man walking. That made him even more dangerous when murdered, so many unresolved issues and regrets, fuel for future hauntings.

I had to stop it.

It feinted right, then headed straight for me. Its darkness surrounded me, oily and off-putting, a disgusting sensation. Still my mate hovered behind me, making me call upon all the strength I possessed. I forced the spirit back, snarling and biting and clawing at the entity.

It could not win.

My fur bristling and electrified, I continued my onslaught. Inch by inch I drove it away until it finally dissipated into a gray mist. Then the particles drifted downward and sunk into the ground, released back to the soil. It didn't have to be that way. I shook my massive head. They could have headed for the light. Instead, they'd never get the opportunity to be reborn. A tragedy. Too late for redemption.

I turned to find my mate staring at me with the biggest bluest eyes I've ever had the pleasure to see, her hair a golden halo in the sunlight. Yes, the visions were spot on.

She reached out and touched my shoulder in reverence, her expression almost disbelieving of what she was seeing. She stroked my fur and it brought me away from the sadness of losing the two tortured souls.

I shifted back, re-dressed and grabbed Esme's arm, loading her into the waiting Mercedes.

"Wow, that was something," Esme said in a thoughtful tone, slumping back on the seat. She glanced at me from under those lovely thick eyelashes with an odd look I couldn't decipher.

"Why did you not get into the limo when I told you to? When danger's near, you need to take better care, lass." I drummed my fingers on my thigh. I itched to take her into my arms and love that annoying distance between us clear away. But even my astounding urge to be inside of her had to be tempered with the knowledge she was not going to take that well. She was her own woman. And while a part of me admired her for it, another part screamed at me to keep her safe.

Who would win this war? Me, no doubt, but I would need to reconvene my forces, align them with the universe, for this was not eighth century Highlands. Much as I wished I could just bear her away to my castle and keep her at my side until she recognized how right we were for each other. I did realize I was pushing her too hard, but I couldn't seem to stop myself.

She looked like she was going to say something else before giving a sigh, then lobbing over a missile. "Just so you know, soon as the police get the real murderer, I'm heading back to my apartment."

I remained silent. I might compromise on some things, but *never* would I consent to her being anywhere but under my roof. I knew where she lived, in a less that luxury apartment block with her friend Meghan. She was not going back there. And I was having Meghan moved to an upscale condo I had purchased for her. As soon as she arrived home today, she'd find the keys and deed of ownership on the kitchen counter.

"How about a dram? You need it and so do I."

I poured us each a good measure of Macallan Lalique from the liquor cabinet and handed one to her. She took it without arguing and we both took a gulp of the fine single malt. It relieved the pressure of the day, settling warm and inviting in my stomach. I gave a sigh of satisfaction.

"Don't you have a show to do for the casino?" she asked, checking me out from the opposite side of the limo as she took another good gulp of Macallan's.

I shrugged and poured us more of the smooth but strong whiskey. What was that old expression, *candy is nice but liquor is quicker?* When I was inside her, I was right where I was supposed to be. Only wolves can experience such an intense connection. Esme was in denial of what was going on between us. Didn't seem to realize that she was mine, and I was hers. That we'd be connected in body and spirit and soul forevermore.

I adopted a nonchalance I wasn't feeling. "I've rearranged things — star's prerogative. Though I will do a performance for my family when they arrive tomorrow."

She downed the second glass of spirits then shook her head at a refill. When she licked her lips, either from nervousness or desire, my wolf stood up and began to pace. The adrenaline rush from our earlier encounter was still in high gear and would take time to totally dissipate.

Soon. We must be clever, let the she-wolf have her space. The last thing I wanted was to drive Esme away. But in the heat of desire, my control was slipping. How long could I keep myself from acting on my pent-up desires?

The limo pulled in front of my new mansion and we disembarked. Esme scooted ahead of me, texting on her phone like her life depended on it. The delicious scent of her arousal wafted back at me as her sundress swayed enticingly around her long tan legs.

"You want to keep yourself safe from me, Esme, go and have a cold shower," I advised.

She turned and gave me a wide-eyed look, then scurried inside the huge front door with the brass knocker fashioned in the shape of a fierce lion's head. That, too, would need changing.

Inside, the head housekeeper greeted us in turn. Ms. Gordon, a woman in her early forties, came with impeccable qualifications. Her smart dress and smoothly styled updo pronounced her a professional and reassured she was up to the heavy responsibilities of keeping my household running smoothly. I had no doubt she could handle all the extra employees that now worked for me.

"Good evening, sir…madam. I've seen to the list of requirements you texted. The master suite is prepared. If you need anything else, please ask."

"I need a room as far from *him* as possible," Esme said, pointing me out like I was chump change. It was all I could do not to take that cheeky lass over my knee and teach her a valuable lesson.

Ms. Gordon was too well educated to allow anything she was thinking to show in her confident expression. "Of course, madam."

"Call me Esme, please."

The woman gave me a look to check if that was fine with me. I nodded my unsmiling approval. "See to it that she has everything her heart desires."

Esme hurried off with the formidable Ms. Gordon in tow while I appreciated the view she created from behind. Did she realize she swayed her hips when she walked? Was that deliberate, meant to capture all my attention? Because it did.

I texted my team, checking for the latest update. Robbie, the lead investigator, immediately answered.

Bad news. The item found in the locker was a vial of morphine. The same substance that the murderer used to kill Danny McCoy. The medical examiner has confirmed the substance in the syringe. A lethal dose of morphine. Explains why his breathing stopped so quickly with his bad ticker.

I let out a string of expletives. Someone was going to a lot of trouble to frame my woman. Why? Over an unpaid bill? It hardly seemed likely. Or was she just an easy target?

Esme

I followed Ms. Gordon to the far end of the mansion, the heat left over from the liquor and sitting beside his nibs all the way home warming me. I couldn't wait to put some distance between him and temptation. Give in to that now and I would regret it, I was certain. Lachlan had to learn that I was no pushover, ready to make love to him at a moment's notice, even though I wanted to.

I had to say, taking a look around to keep my mind out of the bedroom as we walked down the hallway, the place did beat the Hatfield & McCoy hotel all to hell for pure luxury. Obviously, no expense had been spared. The scent of furniture polish and fragrant flowers stirred the senses. Was that fresh heather? And definitely gardenias. My olfactory sense seemed to be getting keener.

"Here you are, Esme...pretty name, by the way. Anything in particular you require? I'll have your wardrobe and other things brought here directly."

Right. Lachlan had overreached and put all my things in his personal living space. I rolled my eyes.

"Men, right! I'm not going to be controlled by a man, no matter how hot he is."

"If you say so." A twinkle came into her gray eyes. She was an attractive woman with dark hair and arresting eyes, her best feature. "But yes, your boyfriend is a hottie. And that kilt, well, that doesn't hurt at all."

"He's not my boyfriend. We're working on a case together." I decided at the last second not to be more specific. I didn't want the staff gossiping about my being involved in a murder investigation. Though they probably already knew. Vegas was like a small town that way. Gossip traveled at the speed of light. News feeds saw to that. Maybe every small city was like that now? Social media had reduced the size of the world to a virtual neighborhood. Good or bad, who really knew?

"Do you know Lachlan well?" I asked, curious.

"No, he hired me through an agency. Most of the staff are new. He had some regulars with him from Creigbourne that help with his show."

"Creigbourne?"

"His castle in the Highlands. You didn't know of it?"

My slow burn sparked to a flash fire in an instant. B & B, right! What other things had he not shared with me? He was far too rich. Guys like that, they had expectations that the female would just fall into line. Oh, that was *not* going to happen.

"No, he neglected to mention that fact," I said through gritted teeth.

"Hmm, well it doesn't make him any less attractive. Always fancied a man with a castle."

"Well, have at it."

She gave me an assessing look. "It might not be my place to say, but all I've heard from his older staff have been good things about Mr. Lachlan Creig. A big-hearted employer who cares about those who work for him."

"Yeah, big of him."

"Will there be anything else?" Her cool tone induced guilt.

"No, thank you. I'm fine. Sorry I was rude, just been an off day." Was I really fine? No, I was a mess. And Mr. Macho Wolf was at the heart of it.

She left and I locked the suite door, needing time to sort myself out.

What was going on at the museum? That was my first worry. Had they found anything significant in that vial they'd found while searching my locker? All that I kept in my assigned space was some work-related stuff. If anything else turned up, then I would tell them the truth…someone had planted it.

I called Meghan on my cell, to see if she knew anything.

"No, but I'll check around. But the craziest thing has just happened!"

"What's that?" I put my face up close to a lovely bouquet of snow-white gardenias and inhaled the awesome scent. Okay, so it didn't totally suck to have someone providing such luxuries.

"Lachlan bought me a condo and I'm standing in it right now. Watch this." She crowed, sending me an instant video of what she was seeing on her end.

What the hell. Now he's trying to buy my friends?

"Isn't it amazing!" The video spun around dizzily as Meghan began to dance about.

My mind spun with the knowledge, but I had to be happy for my friend. She'd never had it easy and lived for periods of doing without even non-luxury necessities to live the life she wanted, without the restraints that selling out could bring. I couldn't begrudge her such a gift. But someone else was going to hear about it.

When she realized I was silent, she spoke, "It's okay if I accept this, right? You won't be upset or anything, Esme?"

"No, of course not. Enjoy it. Not often such a thing happens in a lifetime. Like a waitress or waiter getting a huge tip. But call me if you find out anything about the locker search."

"Sure thing. I'm going to throw a housewarming party soon. Oh, it's going to be so much fun!"

I hung up after reassuring Meghan everything was fine. Maybe I was worrying unnecessarily. Antsy, I wandered over to the window and stared out at the view that was lost on me. One thought intruded. I should go to the police. Stop this thing in the bud. No way they could have found anything that incriminated me. And if they did, I could just say it didn't belong to me. They could check for fingerprints or something like that. Of course, it meant I would need to be fingerprinted, but I was innocent, so that shouldn't matter.

And if I didn't go to the police and they discovered where I was hiding out, then what? I didn't want to imagine how Lachlan would take it if they turned up on his doorstep. He was too macho, too alpha to let them question his she-wolf. And whether I liked it or not, that was how he saw me. I had no idea how to deal with that.

Yes, we were ridiculously compatible on a sexual level, but everywhere else, all we seemed to do was butt heads. Mind you, we'd done well working together at the haunting today, saving a family from having to vacate their home. An excellent turn of events.

Yes. I decided I needed to have a talk with those two detectives. But first a long, long hot shower and something to eat. It had been a hell of a day and I was famished.

Thirty minutes later and I was ready to face the world again, sweet-smelling and dressed in fresh clothing. When I'd emerged from the humongous bathroom I'd found a closetful of endless choices for outfits, and finally settled on black yoga pants and a stretchy purple top that promised comfort and lowkey fashion. Lacing on a pair of sporty red tennis shoes, I threw my hair up into a high ponytail and swiped on some pink lip gloss.

I opened the ensuite refrigerator and pulled out a bottle of water and a prepared cheese, cold meats and fruit plate. *Okay, having an army of servants doesn't exactly suck either.* I set the platter of food on a table overlooking the backyard and plunked myself down in an easy chair. Downing half the water and munching on some of the delicious fruit, I studied the surroundings visible through the large picture window.

The full moon was just rising over a yard lit by an array of old-fashioned black-painted streetlamps every twenty feet, featuring a curved path out to a stepped rise of white tiered rock. The path that disappeared into the distance was set inside a lovely garden with beds of colorful perennials and fruit trees laden with produce. An infinity pool gleamed at the western edge and a tennis court rose to the east. *Not too shabby.*

I stared at the brightness of the moon, sensing its ancient mystery tugging on my soul. I envied those of my kind that would shift under its sway tonight, wishing it were different.

How I long to be a wolf…

Glancing in the full-length mirror standing in an ornate wooden frame nearby, I caught a flash of bright blue reflected back at me. Then it vanished and I was left with ordinary me. Strange. I ate a bit of the cheese, then placed the food back in the fridge. Swigging the last of the water, I tossed the plastic container in a recycling bin hidden in the wall, then pushed open one of the French doors that led onto the back patio.

Taking in invigorating deep breaths of cool air so satisfying after the heat of a scorching summer day in Vegas, I raised my arms over my head and stretched out my spine. My clothes felt itchy to my skin and I scratched at my arms. Was I allergic to the fabric, or something I just ate? My skin felt ready to break out in hives.

A sudden movement to my right and I caught a streak of gray fur racing along the path, then vanishing over the raised stone path in the distance. *Lucky dog. Damn it.* Now I was overheating, like my flesh was on fire. I tore off the offending top, leaving on my sports bra. No obvious red welts suggested the cause for the annoying sensation. Sweat began to trickle down my collarbone. I tugged off my runners and yoga pants, unable to handle the close touch of tight elastic fabric.

A howl in the distance electrified me. The moon seemed brighter now, calling to me in a more distracting way. Who had run out down the path and vanished into the desert? My heart said it was Lachlan. *Convenient having the mansion built outside Vegas, allowing for a special privacy that living in the city couldn't.* I imagined running along that awesome path with another wolf, checking out the lay of the land. If only...

Then the world began to shimmer in front of my eyes.

Chapter Twenty-Three

Esme

The moon vanished from view for a split second as the world over-brightened and I couldn't make out distinct shapes, like a mirage floating on the over-heated desert floor at high noon. A strange sense of disconnect bored into me before the entire world vanished before my very eyes. Frightened, I tried hanging on, all my senses tingling as something fired through my bloodstream, leaving chaos in its wake. I was being torn apart and I had no idea why or what to do. I froze in panic, unable to understand what was happening to me.

Was I having a seizure of some kind? A stroke? Then my vision cleared and I gave a chuff of relief. *A chuff?* I tried to speak but all that came out was a low growl. Looking down, I realized the ground was closer. Much closer than it should be if I were still standing.

Oh my goddess! I had paws. Fur. Thick gray-brown fur like my pack. I had shifted to wolf, my innermost dream come true. The overhead light seemed too bright and I padded to the edge of the fancy brick patio. Then I took off down the path at a smooth lope, my new form seeming to understand how it all worked without any prompting from me, knowing instinctively how to run with four legs instead of two. The cool night of the land beckoned to me, the mishmash of scents begging to be discovered enthralling me. Freedom.

The ancient moon lit the way as I left the path behind at the top of the tiered steps of white rock and took off across the sand dunes, the land warm beneath my paws. I howled at the starlit sky, my ghostly ancestors racing alongside me in the periphery of my vision. At an artesian well, I lapped up the water. I searched out new fragrances, my nose too busy to bother with watching all that closely where I was going — I just had to go!

I was intoxicated with this new state of being, ready to take on the world. I ran for miles and miles. Then, drunk with happiness, I lay down with my belly on the sand near a Joshua tree. My tongue lolled from the exertion, my muscles relaxing after the burn of exercise. This was paradise. Almost as good as bedding Lachlan. No, this *had* to be as good as bedding that uber-alpha — I had been wishing for it my entire life. For the first time I didn't feel less-than and it was amazing. Could I do this again? I had kind of fallen into it this time, but surely, with practice, it would become second nature?

The scent of another wolf drifted past my muzzle and I brought up my head, checking the wind for confirmation. I recognized the macho fragrance and growled deep in my throat. Sure, it had been him leading the way earlier, loping across the backyard.

I stood my ground, waiting for him to come to me.

Lachlan

The enticing scent of my mate led me directly to her hiding spot under the Joshua tree. She watched me approach as I strutted my stuff before her. Her blue eyes blazed with mystery, her fur thick and rich with blonde streaks that matched her hair color as human. *Magnificent.* A worthy Forever Mate if ever there was one. I was proud of her. She'd finally shifted and I had no small part in that, having blessed her with my bite. Surely she'd see reason now that she knew the full score and not take such offense that I'd jumped the gun and claimed her.

I moved to lie down beside her, nipping the back of her neck playfully. She growled. Why was she warning me? I was her Forever Mate.

Ye shifted, my caileag ghrinn.

I'm wolf now, not a lass.

She looked at me then with those huge blue eyes that glittered in the moonlight, a deep liquid well of ancient understanding. She'd come around, she had to. I just needed to give her time.

We lay side by side under the tree. It was a special moment. The first time my mate had ever shifted. Soon enough the rest of the Luceres would know. We'd invite everyone to our handfasting. Unite two powerful clans. *Just a matter of time, right?* Unease filled me at what I couldn't control, even with all the money in the world. The outcome of the investigation against my mate loomed large. Hard as I pressed for answers, still they eluded me. Eluded my team.

No, proof was needed before the law came after her again. My unease just stemmed from the timing, I reassured myself. I didn't want Esme to go through an unwarranted interrogation before the real murderer was set down before them, gift wrapped in guilt for the two detectives heading the case. Just thinking of it made my fur stand on end.

I rose in agitation and shook off the annoying feeling no alpha would ever admit to.

Time to go back – it's late.

Go ahead.

So, she was going to be just as feisty as a wolf. Much as I admired it, right now I needed cooperation, not attitude.

It's safer inside once the moon reaches its zenith. Other wolves are prowling about, and I can't leave you here. They may attack an unaccompanied female. And I need to work on this investigation. I have calls to make.

She gave me a look that screamed defiance. Then she slowly stretched and got to her feet, trying my patience as she sent me one taunting word.

Whatever.

We trotted back toward the mansion, the moon to our back, lighting the way home. There would be many such opportunities in the future, but only one short window of time to fix the present fiasco. But my mate shifting, that loomed large in making my day, giving me more patience to deal with her less-than-respectful attitude.

I escorted her back onto the patio in front of her suite, then followed her inside.

What do you think you're doing? she asked, her legs stiffening with displeasure as she stood her ground.

I need to shift and borrow some clothes. Plausible.

She waited.

Me first? I asked.

She nodded, her eyes glittering. This would be her first time changing back to human and I wanted to make sure it went smoothly. Be there for her. *She is my inspiration, my battle cry.*

I sent out my request to the universe and the portal to the realm next door opened up. In a split second I stepped through the wavering shield of light and came back a man.

"Now you, Esme," I said.

She shimmered in front of me for a moment as I held my breath, praying it went well for her. Sparks of fierce light emanating from the breach in the multiverse followed her request to shift, then a second later she too stood there in all her naked glory. A woman.

And what a woman! A goddess among women, all curves and lush skin. Though I loved her wolf form, I loved this more.

We stared at each other. I drank in her beauty. Her grace.

I moved first, but she wouldn't give in to her obvious lust, holding herself stiff and away from me. It was costing her though. The scent, the warmth, the urgent need, all struck me in the loins as it did her. I throbbed with the extreme urge to mate with her and her body trembled, holding on by a thread.

"No! Not until you promise me."

"Anything." I lay my hands on her soft shoulders, breathed in her intoxicating scent, my nostrils flaring.

"You have to let me be free, to come and go without you or anyone on your team of hired hands following me. You do that, and we'll begin again."

"Bit late for that."

She grew stiller still.

"Yes, of course, whatever you want. Come and go as you like. Just please wait until the investigation is completed and we have proof of guilt."

"No. Now. Promise me, cross your heart?"

I ignored the pleading in her eyes that was making me uncomfortable and held out my pinky. "Pinky swear — good enough for ye?"

"That will do. Now, come here, my big bad wolf."

Then all talking came to a halt as we allowed the lust that had been building to escape.

I swept her into my arms, uncaring about anyone or anything on the planet. Life would intervene soon enough. Right now, I had the green light from my Forever Mate and we needed to celebrate our union.

This moment was going to be even better than the first time I had been with Esme, amazing as that had been, for this time around, knowing that we were chosen one for the one, this would be the best it could be. A no-holds-barred-fated-wolf mating, which was the headiest on earth.

"I'm going to love you every way possible, all night long, until you can't take it anymore. Bind you to me," I promised, a low-pitched thrumming resonating in my tone.

She swallowed, then stared me in the eyes. The musty odor of sex permeated the room. "Good. I want that. I want you, all of you."

I stood naked and proud, my huge cock jutting upward, the immense size nudging the apex of her thighs. "I need your permission, Esme, before I can't control myself anymore. For the knotting, lass?"

"Yes."

The single word resonated through me, sending my libido skyward. "I'm going to taste you. God, your scent is like flowers and honey." I slipped my fingers between her thighs, touching her pussy, pulling the lips apart.

I picked her up in my arms and laid her on the bed. I swept my tongue down her channel in one full sweep.

She shuddered, arching off the bed. Pleasure had to be pushing her hard in tight waves, making her throb visibly, making me all the harder. I teased her, using my thumb to lightly circle her clit, pushing a thick finger inside her, then adding a second one that made her moan aloud and thrash her head back and forth, caught in a whirlwind of sensations.

"You taste of sweet life," I growled, knowing her essence glistened on my lips. "But I need to be inside you." I rubbed my lips with the back of my hand.

"Hurry, I need you. Now," she urged.

The intense look on her face warmed something deep inside me, something powerful. It sizzled to life as the power of her gaze spread throughout my body.

I stared down at her. "You are so beautiful, open to me like that. Heavens above, you make me humbled at the magnificence of the universe, bringing us together."

Esme

Lachlan grabbed his cock as if to emphasize his words. My gaze took in the picture he made, a Viking-Wulver warrior looming before me, his cock huge and arresting. I melted into a puddle of want. And lust. And heat.

"Now, before I expire."

The stark words hung between us for an instant— piercing, vibrating, making me aware of life as I had never experienced it before. He fell on me hungrily after that slight moment of realization, of hesitation, as if there were no tomorrow. He used his fingers to separate my labia, thrusting his cock into me without preamble. I was more than ready, opening to him, farther than I had imagined possible. His deep thrusts pushed me to the edge, making the drive for release almost painful in its intensity. The pleasure-pain drove me onward, searching, seeking, yearning…

"Yes! Just like that. Hard! Harder!" I gripped his ass with my fingers, my legs spread wide as he pumped into me. "Don't stop."

He obliged my entreaties, continuing for long precious moments, sweat dripping, unimaginable heat coursing through me. The wild sounds of flesh slapping against flesh, salty and alive. Alive. The word seared my brain and drove me to new heights. I pushed against him, lost in the sensation of powerful, mind-blowing sex. Over and over again.

Then he swelled inside me, so huge we locked in place. The slight discomfort turned to exquisiteness as we rocked against each other, unable to do anything but be held in its sway. Long incredible moments passed.

An eternity. Of pure. Unleashed. Pleasure.

"I can't hold off any longer," he warned finally. "Come for me, Esme. I need you to come for me."

My mind absorbed his words, allowing me to finally fall over the edge. I set myself free at that moment, slipped away from bonds, slipped away from anything but being there. With him.

His body jerked a few times, his hips bucking against mine. He fell on top of me, both of us exhausted, breathing heavily, our hot sweaty bodies pressed together.

"That was unbelievable," he murmured, his eyes glowing as he stared down at me. He turned on his side to draw me close.

"It was," I agreed when I could find my breath and regain my senses. My lips curled upward into a smile.

"I like that," he said. He traced my mouth with a finger.

"What?"

"That smile. You need to smile more often."

I stared into his eyes, seeing my own reflection hovering over his soul in the incredibly bright green depths that stirred my own. "Nice to have something to smile about."

"You need to be made love to often...every day. I can see that now."

"I won't disagree with that assessment." I trailed my fingers down his chest, the smooth skin warm and firm under my fingertips. "But I can see you need it just as badly." He was already hard again, his cock rising between his muscled thighs.

"Good thing we've got all night." An unspoken agreement between us to stay in the moment simmered under the surface, freeing me to be myself, to reach out to him with all I possessed. He grasped my breast, circling the hardening nipple with a thumb and forefinger, gently tugging on it. His actions sent tingles of pleasure to my pussy, arousing me. How could I still need more of this man? It defied reason. But there was proof as my channel clenched anew, flowing with moisture again.

"Good thing." I reached up and stroked his cheek. "My turn to pleasure you."

"Let me wash up first," he said, slipping out of bed. He was back. Fast.

I got onto my knees and tugged him to the bed with an outstretched hand, positioning myself between his thighs. I gave him a half-smile, grasped him at the base of his cock, then proceeded to lick and kiss and suck my way down the thick shaft and over his balls. His deep groans of pleasure were all the thanks I needed while applying myself with utter dedication to my self-appointed task.

Lachlan swept my hair back from my face, watching me. The more I caressed him, the hotter the moment became.

"So incredible. That's it," he said, fisting my hair, his balls and his cock throbbing in undulating waves, giving over to the expected release of his hot cum. My throat worked to swallow it all and I knew he immediately wanted me again. Never had I imagined being so in tune with a man. Never had I wanted to make love to a man over and over again until he was completely mine.

I was so ready and wet and willing.

It scared me, far worse than anything else in this world, to find a man accepting me for who I was, to feel such intensity vibrating in my tiny body as he thrust his cock inside me without question. It was beyond amazing. Maybe this kind of intensity would burn itself out by morning. Or maybe not ever…

"I don't know it could be like this, the stuff of myths and legends." He tucked a curl behind my ear.

"Me neither."

"Rest now, my love."

But we never did that night, the sun coming up before our bodies gave in to exhaustion.

Chapter Twenty-Four

Esme

I woke disorientated, finding myself alone, before the night's wonderous adventures came flooding back. I had been a wolf. I had made love to a man that could not get enough of me over and over. A man who promised to respect my boundaries. It did not get better than that.

I checked the time to find it already mid-morning and scurried out of bed, in a hurry to shower. I wanted to clear my slate, end the outside problem with the police and spend more time with Lachlan. His family was coming today after all, and I wanted things to be easy between us, not have something hanging over our heads.

What to wear took a few vital moments of indecision. What does one wear to a police interrogation? The color white for purity or black to hide stains if I rubbed up against something I shouldn't have? I ended up choosing a simple navy-blue dress with ballet flats and little ornamentation. I wanted to be taken seriously.

I opened the fridge to find a fresh platter of fruit and cheese. Croissants, donuts, and other pastries were piled high on a plate near the single coffee maker. Brewing a nice dark roast, I quickly consumed enough calories to get me through the day, keeping an eye out for any movement in the backyard. A gardener was working on the flower beds, weeding.

Okay, time to hit the road. I left a note for Lachlan, then slipped out of the front door, pleased that I had managed the feat without being stopped by the staff or coming upon Loki, who might have given the game away. I wanted this over with.

I stopped in my tracks, staring. Wow. A classy silver-colored Mercedes sports car was parked at the curb, a big red bow encircling it with my name stenciled on the banner. Aww, he had thought of everything. What a man.

I jumped in the driver's seat and sped off. Time to reclaim my life. My life felt charmed as I parked in the lot at the Vegas Police Department Remand Center. All I needed to do was explain myself to them, show I wasn't hiding anything, and the door to the rest of my life would open wide.

Hurrying up the front stone steps of the three-story building, I stopped to appreciate the cement planters of colorful fragrant flowers someone had taken the time to make and place there. Inside the air-conditioned police station, I orientated myself, then strode across the floor to the reception desk.

"Hello, I was wondering if I could speak with Detective Tom Olson or his partner Sean Jackson?"

The desk sergeant gave me a quick assessing look over his bifocals. "What's this about?"

"About a case they're working on. I'm Esme Luceres and I was the tour guide the night that Danny McCoy was found dead. I'm here to answer any questions they may have."

The desk sergeant startled, then quickly regained his composure. "Okay, come with me. Right this way, miss." He rose to his feet and beckoned me to follow him.

I did, right down a wide hallway with some of the officers giving me interested looks, and into a small room.

"Please, wait here. Someone will be with you directly."

"Pretty good service, thanks," I remarked as he quickly closed the door on a very tiny room. Not to mention plain and dingy. The place could really use sprucing up. Some color wouldn't go amiss on those off-white, visibly scarred walls. I didn't want to imagine some of the things that had been seen and heard in this dismal room.

Less than a minute later, the detectives trooped in, grim-faced and official. I didn't appreciate the suspicion obvious in both pairs of eyes that accused me of unimaginable things.

I swallowed my concern, smiling brightly. A smile no one returned. "Morning, Detectives. I've come voluntarily to answer any questions you may still have about that dreadful night."

They shared a glance and I wished nervously that I could read human minds.

"Is your lawyer here?" Detective Olson asked.

"No, I came on my own. I imagined by now you have discovered the connection between Albert Caltrain and his brother Vinny?"

"We're looking into it and we can't discuss any more than that with you. I'm more interested in what you have to say, Miss Luceres, about how the vial with residue of morphine we found in your locker came to be there?"

"Someone planted it, obviously," I said, my smile vanishing.

The detective didn't bite, but pursed his lips. "Were you having an affair with Danny McCoy? His wife seems to think so."

"What? An affair?" I shook my head, shocked at the accusation. "Never. I hardly knew the man. It was weeks ago we debunked his having a ghost in his hotel. Since then, other than sending out an invoice or two for the work my team did for him, I've had no further contact with him."

"No contact at all? Then how do you explain this lovey-dovey little card from him that we found in your costume you wear at the museum?"

"What card?" I glanced at the damning evidence encased in a plastic sheath. "I can't explain that—I've never seen it before. Someone else had to have slipped it into my pocket. Maybe the person who broke into my locker to leave the evidence? They could have done it."

"So you say."

I began to chew on my thumbnail. "I've never seen that before. You have to believe me." *Damn it. Looks like I should have protected myself better. Safety 101.* But it just never occurred to me. I'm a Luceres, a shifter, though only other shifters know that. It had been a huge mistake in hindsight to think I was invincible because of my bloodline.

"Besides, Danny was there with his current girlfriend. She's as likely to be involved as not. Have you looked into her?"

"She's cooperating fully. While you, Miss Luceres, have been hard to reach."

"I didn't know you were looking for me." I swallowed, realizing I had just spoken a lie. The cold eyes boring into mine from across the table made me cringe.

"Do I need a lawyer?" I asked, sitting up straighter.

"Do you think you need a lawyer?"

"Only if you're going to pin this on me. I didn't do it. I didn't have anything to do with Danny McCoy's death." I shook my head vehemently. "Nothing at all. I'm sorry for what happened to him, but you've got the wrong person in this room. You should be out investigating Albert and Vinny Caltrain. Have you even uncovered the bodies in the house we de-ghosted yesterday? They're hidden under the floor, under the barrels."

"And a ghost told you all that?" Detective Olson gave a snort.

"And yet you couldn't find a ghost for Danny McCoy at his hotel," Detective Jackson finally put in his piss-poor two words.

"That's because there wasn't one there! I can't find what doesn't exist, Detective!" Exasperated at their short-sightedness, I felt the familiar burn of temper rise up. When my wolf growled, I put a lid on it, though it wasn't easy. That would be the last thing I needed to have happen, my anger unleashing my newly discovered and fierce wolf who didn't know the rules yet. All of the shifter kingdom would descend and chew me a new one.

"So, what we do have is a vial of morphine, a card from the victim to you, and an anonymous person discussing how angry you were with Danny McCoy, and a woman who had the means and opportunity."

"My prints aren't on the vial...they can't be, or the card. You can test for that, surely?"

"You consent to fingerprinting?"

"And a lie detector. I have nothing to hide. Nothing at all. And once you dig up those bodies, you'll agree. You have a serial killer on your hands and you're sitting here talking to me! That's a big waste of time, Detective."

He narrowed his eyes at me, his lips a thin line, his nostrils flaring. I didn't care, I had to push this cretin to get on with things. That was obvious now.

"We know how to do our jobs, Miss Luceres."

"If you did, you'd have the real suspect hauled in here and have all your answers in no time!" My neck was getting too warm, perspiration dampening the back of my hair. My hands trembled with anger mingled with a touch of fear. If I couldn't persuade them to get onto the right course of action, this day was doomed to not go the way I envisioned.

"Am I free to go?" I wasn't hanging around for any more of this abuse. My wolf was being held inside by the thinnest of threads, threatening to expose my pack.

A loud commotion resounded nearby, taking up the full attention of everyone in the room. The two detectives leaped to their feet, slamming the door on their way out.

Stymied, I got up from the uncomfortable chair. What was that about? Did a suspect confess more easily when seated in such a torture device?

My cell rang and I answered it without looking at the number, distracted by listening to what was going on outside the room.

"Where are you?" Cristaldo asked in a tone of voice that sent chills skittering down my spine.

"Uh, the police station." I began to chew on a fingernail, wishing I had declined the call. This might get ugly.

"Is Lachlan there with you?"

"No, why should he be?"

A huge sigh of frustration. "He's supposed to be keeping his eye on you. I'm coming. Don't say anything else until I arrive."

The phone went dead in my hand. Cristaldo had asked Lachlan to look after me like I was some kind of charity case? Red-hot anger twisted my guts.

I stormed from the room and into the front area. *Goddamn it.* I should have known. Lachlan Creig stood there in all his warrior glory, berating the desk sergeant and anyone else in earshot.

I was angry at the world by the point, angry at the insanity of my current predicament, angry that he had fooled me once more, believing he would let me be free of such interventions and following me around like I was some kind of idiot. I might be a lesser Luceres, at least until now that I had unexpectedly learned to shift, but I could take care of myself. I always had. I didn't need a man telling me what to do or looking out for me. Especially one that had been asked to by Cristaldo. Was that all this was? His needing to keep an eye out for me? All my insecurities came flooding back, bringing a storm of fire with them. I was no longer in control of myself or anything else.

I stomped right up to him.

"Quit. Stalking. Me. Now!" I shouted.

He blanched at the harsh words I'd hurled at him. The anger seemed to leach right out of his face, his arms that had been raised to berate the officer dropping to his side.

"Esme…" He said the one word, then seemed to think better of saying anything more. He turned and vanished out of the door of the police station, shocking me to the core. *What?* Why would he do that? Sure, I was angry, angry as hell. My temper had a way of getting away from me. But his response was not what I expected. Okay…well…at least he'd stopped arguing with the desk sergeant.

"Miss Luceres." Detective Tom Olson strode up to me, his expression grim enough to sour cream. I had even less patience for him.

Lachlan

Oh my God, had I stepped over the line with Esme? Been *stalking* her like she'd accused me of? We'd been so close last night, connected as only Forever Mates could be, *then this*? She'd stared at me with pure fury in her eyes. Worse yet, her wolf had threatened to expose her. I'd had to leave. She might have broken the most important were rule of all—*keep the pack safe*.

I stopped at the limo parked at the curb to let my brothers know I needed to clear my head, walk around for a while. My pack had arrived only an hour earlier and I'd brought them along as reinforcements, in case the situation went south. Instead, it had gone directly to hell.

"Lachlan, you okay?" Calan asked, his eyes assessing me, sharing a look with Logan. "Everything go all right with Esme?"

"Aye, but I need to work a few things out. I'll join you at the house soon. Go and look after the clan, make sure everyone has what they need? I won't be long."

"Sure, of course, bro. Just don't take too long. We've got lots to catch up on."

I watched the limousine drive away, proud I had managed to keep it all together when my heart had just been broken. *How had it all gone so wrong since last night?*

I stumbled off down the street, passing casinos and hotels without noticing where I was headed. Mary had once accused someone of stalking her. A horrifying situation that had turned nasty and tragic. But I could never hurt my beloved. How could my Forever Mate think so poorly of me? To throw that horrible word right in my face. How could I have been so wrong, so misguided?

If Esme thought that of me...that I was capable of stalking her when all I wanted to do was keep her safe, well, then I had to face the fact that the future had changed. Maybe there was to be no happy ending for us. A quick handfasting, then a life spent together — the dream might have just ended with that one word.

A quick intake of breath as the worst pain of my life seared through me. Where to go from here? I needed my country, suddenly craving the isolation of Creigbourne more than anything else on earth. A place to be, maybe to heal, if such a thing were even possible...

Chapter Twenty-Five

Esme

Why did Lachlan follow me after I expressly told him how angry that made me? I had been vague about the errand I had to run, so he had to have been watching me, just like Cristaldo had asked him to. He had promised not to do that again, but I had another twinge of unease at the memory of the devastated look on his face, hating that I had been responsible for putting it there.

I took a quick look around the parking lot of the police department as I exited the building. I was darned happy to be free of the detectives and their insinuations and questions, at least for now. I had been warned again not to leave town. *As if.*

I wished suddenly that I could catch a glimpse of that handsome Scotsman in the daring kilt waiting for me, but the lot was nearly deserted. I could have been a bit nicer, not screamed at him. I did need to work on controlling my temper better. But darn it, he had to learn, right? But maybe I too had a lot to figure out if I wanted to become a better person. I shook off the ominous feeling that something was really, really wrong, that had my stomach roiling with unease.

Where would he go? *Yes, he probably went back to the mansion to be with his family.* They were scheduled to arrive this morning and it was now mid-afternoon. The fingerprinting and other useless pursuits had taken up precious time. I needed to see him face-to-face, explain how important it was that he never do that again, come riding to my rescue when I didn't need him to. Not if we had any hope of making it as a couple.

I jumped into my sporty new car and tore back to the mansion, pedal to the metal all the way as I sang along at the top of my lungs to a favorite tune playing on the DVD, my way of dealing with stress. I needed to sing that loathsome experience in that tiny interrogation room right out of my body. And maybe even more importantly if I would but admit it, that distressed look on Lachlan's face.

But nothing worked. I couldn't get the raw pain I'd seen on his face out of my mind. It twisted me up, made me feel like the villain. A sinking feeling made me think maybe I was in this case.

After parking the car, I hurried into the impressive foyer, expecting the place to be lively with Creigs and clansmen, with maybe a bagpipe or two being played. Instead, it was quiet. Too quiet. Maybe they had all gone to the casino to get ready for Lachlan's show tonight?

I hurried into the massive Great Room and found a large group of people sitting and standing around, speaking in quiet little groups. A mix of generations, their solemness was a surprise. I'd have thought coming to Vegas for a show to see a relative perform as well as their host did would have them in high spirits. I took a good look around but couldn't spot Lachlan anywhere. I'd been so certain he'd be in attendance, cavorting with his fellow clansmen.

I smiled brightly and greeted the room with a cheerful, "Hello, everyone. I'm Esme, of the House of Luceres. I look forward to meeting and speaking with all of you in turn." I surprised myself by announcing the connection to my pack, but now that I could shift, I felt a bit better about belonging. The stab of realization that in some way Lachlan had helped me to do that didn't help with the guilt. It was getting harder to shake off by the moment.

A lot of heads swiveled my way. I heard a few whispered words. I caught a few. *Is that her?* The voice wasn't asking in a flattering way. An older matriarch rose to her feet and with a great deal of dignity made her way over to me. Everyone else held back, as if this was the normal course of things.

"Esme Luceres, I am The Creig of the Highland Wulver Heathens Clan. I tend to announce our names in the old way. Most of the young people don't admit to Wulver anymore," she explained. She reached out and grasped my hands in hers. Her touch held strength, though I was certain from the deep wrinkles and fine white hair she had to be ninety if she were a day.

"Lovely to meet you," I said, giving a small curtsey of acknowledgment of the importance of her rank. That she was the queen she-wolf of her clansmen was obvious from the looks of respect she received from her fellow pack members around the spacious room. Everyone waited now for her to have her say.

"Come, sit by me, child," she said and patted my hands. I dutifully followed her to one of the loveseats circling the huge stone fireplace. A cheerful fire was burning in the grate, a surprising event on a hot Vegas day when air conditioning was the norm.

"I'm always cold. I had the staff start the fire for me," she explained as we sat down close to each other on the gold brocade settee. I noticed then that others were perspiring freely in the room. Give me a few minutes and I'd be joining them. I'd have to shower first before heading out to Lachlan's show.

"I understand. My grandmother's the same way."

"So, ye are to be Lachlan's intended," she said. "Land's sake, I must say yer not exactly what I expected, bless yer heart."

I hid my chagrin at her blunt words with a bit of difficulty. But who challenges an old lady? I even managed to keep the smile on my face. But my confidence meter took a huge hit, not that I was Lachlan's *intended*, though I had no idea really what I was to him. Too soon for me to say. Not until we got past this current hurdle that was standing directly in our path.

"What were you expecting?"

"Well, Lachlan's been through a lot these past years, though he tries to hide it. I thought ye'd be a more, shall I say, calm and understanding type."

Well, that sucked. I thought myself a decent person. "Where is he? I don't see him here."

"He's gone, child. I'd have thought ye'd know that...he took off for parts unknown."

"What! Why?" Stunned, I shot forward in my seat.

"I think ye may know more about this than anyone."

Her wise green-colored eyes bore into mine. I began biting my thumbnail, then stopped as I realized how rude and unladylike it was to do that before the matriarch. "Me? No, sorry, I'm as surprised as anyone."

"Did the two of ye have words today? It's unlike my grandson to leave everyone like this."

My neck grew hotter, from the fire that seemed to be roaring with heat now. "Well, we did have a bit of a situation. I've been telling him not to follow me around...that I can handle myself."

"He's overprotective." Her understanding nod helped me to continue. "Really, *really* overprotective. It drives me crazy. I'm a she-wolf, for heaven's sake, I know how to take care of myself!" I realized my voice was rising from the stress and I bit down on my tongue, the sudden pain helping me to control myself better.

"Counting to ten also helps."

I blushed, knowing she'd called me out proper.

"He did teach me how to shift."

"Ye mean that ye shifted first time with my grandson's help?"

"Right. It was fabulous, almost the best thing ever." I didn't think I should add the bit about how great he and I were in bed. It was a tad inappropriate.

"If ye never shifted before, child, there's only one other way it could have happened." She gave a knowing smile. "Did he bite you?"

"Yes, and I..." I couldn't very well say that he hadn't been given permission, since I kind of did. And it was such a blur now, such an amazing time, that I really wasn't certain any more of the sequence of events.

"Then ye both truly are Forever Mates, destined for bigger and better things. Chosen." She seemed to be thinking of something that took her far away in her mind for a moment while I tried to absorb the impact of her words. No way did it prove that, right?

"Ye don't know about the lovely Mary. Lachlan didn't share her tragic story." It wasn't phrased as a question. Her voice had lowered, as if she didn't want anyone else to hear what she had to say. My curiosity sparked, sensing what she had to tell me was of vital importance.

"Mary? No, nothing." Was the 'lovely Mary' a special person to Lachlan? A flash of green jealousy sliced through my belly, startling in its intensity. The Creig paused, observing me with a frown.

"It's best ye know, child. Ye can't build a life on secrets. It just leads to more pain. Lord knows we've kept this hidden away long enough in our family."

I nodded, needing desperately to understand.

"Mary was betrothed to Lachlan's cousin, Conner. They were Forever Mates, fated to be together, about to be handfasted. Then another alpha wolf, from a distant clan, the MacGregors, decided that Mary was the lass for him. Took to following her around, causing all kinds of havoc. He stalked her, in the bluntest terms possible. His actions were deplorable, evil."

"Oh my goddess, I accused Lachlan of stalking me!" Aghast at my earlier choice of words, I sat stunned, knowing I had made a terrible mistake. What I saw in the old woman's eyes when I admitted that chilled me to the bone. "What happened to Mary?"

"She committed suicide when she wouldn't consent to be with the MacGregor wolf. He kidnapped her one foul night, bore her to a cave in the Highlands. She drowned herself by throwing herself off the cliffs at Creigbourne when he wouldn't let her go. As ye know, no Forever Mate can be long without the other. It's a long, silent, tragic living death for a mate that's left behind. Conner's spirit died with Mary's."

"What do I do now? I must have hurt Lachlan horribly when I accused him of stalking me. I'm so, so sorry. He was probably just trying to help me, keep me safe in the police station. He overreacted, but I admit, I did as well."

"Aye, ye did. It's best to get all the facts before jumping to a conclusion. Anger that comes from insecurity can be tempered." Her eyes took on an otherworldly look as if something ancient were speaking through her. "Self-knowledge is the best power when ye use it to improve yerself. That's all the control we really have, child, whether as human or wolf."

Her gentle chiding made me feel even worse. Sudden heat flooded my body. I couldn't sit still one more second.

I leaped to my feet. "I have to go. I need to find him — explain. Say I'm sorry."

"Aye, child, that ye do. As he does as well for pushing ye too hard. But now at least ye understand." She nodded and slumped back on the sofa, as though reliving the past had exhausted her. "Go, find him at Castle Creigbourne, before it's too late. With his second sight, he'll be in double the pain. And remember, only with taking the biggest chances can one experience the biggest rewards."

Chapter Twenty-Six

Lachlan

If I had any doubt that Esme was my destined Forever Mate, it vanished as the distance between us lengthened, each mile more painful than the last. Thankfully Creigbourne called to me, tugged at my spirit, the only place on earth capable of helping me to live through the nightmare of rejection.

I should have seen all this earlier, I chastised myself. She'd fought me tooth and nail since we'd met. Was that only a few days ago? It seemed a lifetime ago now. From the highest heights to the deepest despair. Actually, the pain was perhaps numbing now, my heart chilling by degrees, turning to stone once more.

Out the cockpit of the Learjet, the mists parted like the gods had a hand in my return, revealing the ancient fortress of Creigbourne. The oldest castle in the Highlands was built of stone, clay soil and oak trees, meant to last a thousand years. And so it had, and hundreds of years more, refurbished as needed, added to when the clan had grown in numbers.

Today it promised sanctuary, if not a place to heal.

I landed the plane then strode through the nearly deserted castle. Regret for letting my clan down, with them having gone all the way to Vegas to see my show, rode me as well. I opened a cupboard and grabbed a full bottle of Macallan, then headed outside to drink it, Loki by my side.

"It's okay, my Loki boy," I reassured my loyal hound. His head kept butting my hand or leg as I slumped down on the stone bench on the edge of the cliff overlooking the deep frigid waters of the loch, the fragrance of heather and the music of birdsong dulled and distant to my mind. Mary had ended her life at this spot. Thrown herself onto the rocks below to avoid the pain of separation from her Forever Mate. I understood now more than ever before, the agony she must have endured. The poor wee lassie.

I drank some more then got to my feet and walked slowly to the very edge of the earth, a few pebbles disturbed by my actions tumbling down to the rocks far below. An eagle flew overhead and circled above me, haunting the brief minutes of twilight, that liminal time when it was best to observe the spirit world. I should open my third eye, check that my reading still held true, but the strength and resolve to do so seemed to have vanished. What was the point of torturing myself further? Esme was lost to me. I had driven my mate away.

Esme

"I need the use of one of our company jets," I demanded, unwilling to back down though my heart beat like the drumline of a marching band. This was unlike me, a person who never wanted the family to know much about me, who stayed and probably proved myself the outsider by my actions alone. That thought riveted me for a moment, realizing how much I had grown since I had met Lachlan.

Cristaldo Luceres narrowed his eyes at me. *A brand-new me.* "What's going on, Esme? You've never wanted my help before. Besides, you can't leave the country right now. The police are still investigating a crime you are a suspect in."

"I never needed your help before. Now I do. And if I'm out of the country, they'll figure out that I had nothing to do with it. It was all a set-up to hide the crimes of others. The real murderer is a serial killer or a serial killer's brother who had to know what was going on, hired most likely by the wife to get an 'instant divorce'. Soon as the police wake up and dig in the basement, they'll find the bodies, proving my assertions."

My earlier concerns over the looming murder case had lessened considerably in light of my worry about Lachlan.

"How did you find out that there are bodies buried in a basement?" Cristaldo's expression was more perplexed than angry now.

"A Ghoststompers, Inc. investigation. Lachlan Creig and I worked on it together." I smiled briefly at the memory of how much we had assisted each other to help the family in need. "The ghosts spoke to Lachlan. He's amazing, a true ghost whisperer. Can I have the jet or not? Otherwise, I'll go book a flight. Nothing's going to stop me from going there. Lachlan needs me."

"No, best to keep this quiet. I'll have a pilot prepared to take you within the hour."

"Thank you."

"Is Lachlan Creig your Forever Mate? You light up when you mention him."

"I think he is. I didn't see it at first—we were always fighting—but now, since I pushed him away, I realize that he's important to my future. He even helped me to shift for the first time."

Cristaldo's eyes widened at learning that important bit of knowledge.

I continued my explanation, "I need to go to him to apologize for things I said that I shouldn't have." That awful scene in the police department played over and over in my head, looking worse by the hour. I had to fix this, praying I wasn't too late in realizing how much he meant to me. Every hour that passed since I'd last seen him was harder to bear. I had to get to him, make this right.

"Fighting and challenges are all part of finding our true path. If Lachlan is your chosen, as it sounds like he is since he's helped you to shift, you need to fight for that. Go. We'll cover for you here. Make sure that the detectives are encouraged to look in the right location."

"Lachlan has a huge team already working on exposing the true murderer. His clan is residing at the legendary Breakers mansion at the moment—they can fill you in on things. Maybe you can all work together? Feed each other information? That would speed things up."

Cristaldo nodded in agreement. "Good thinking. I'll look into that. Esme, I'm glad you're back with us. You've been absent from our family for far too long."

His words softened my heart, for the first time I was happy to have been born a Luceres, even though the worry for Lachlan was eating away at me.

"It's good to be back," I said with a wink, surprising the alpha and perhaps myself even more. And with that I hurried from the penthouse, needing to get to the tarmac and hop on that Learjet headed for the Highlands.

* * * *

The jet, though one of the quickest built by humans, was too slow for me. Something deep down inside me spoke of having no more time. I had to get to Lachlan. Immediately. I had tried to contact him telepathically, sending my thoughts outward to him, but I was blocked by something. What was getting in the way? The more I felt myself hampered from contacting him, the more I realized how much he meant to me. Was I falling for the guy?

Images flickered of meeting him at the billboard in front of the theater, his mere presence sending me into a tailspin, his dancing the tango with me on stage where I had to admit he made me look good, him coming on the ghost tour and handing me a lovely gardenia blossom, pretending to pull it out from behind my ear. When he talked to that spirit in the basement, it darn near blew me away. Then helping with the murder inquiry, sparing no expense. What normal alpha wolf does all that?

Only the magnificent Lachlan.

But it was that special smile I loved most of all. When those bright green eyes lit up as he looked at me, that was what tugged at my heartstrings. I really could see my unborn children in his eyes.

Oh, my goddess. I had fallen for him these past few days. Then driven him away. I felt a knife stab at my heart with the thought of how badly I had hurt an alpha wolf only looking to protect me. He'd been set up by the tragic events of the past, was as much a victim as me.

Please, please, make this goddamn jet fly faster!

Every second was becoming a torture. When I didn't think I could stand it a moment longer, Castle Creigbourne came into view through the portal window. But it was nearly dusk when we finally set down on the private runway a few hundred feet from the castle. Thankfully the runway was big enough to accommodate the jet...and was more proof that Lachlan had money to burn. *Like that matters anymore.*

"Do you want me to wait, Miss Luceres?" the pilot asked, turning to observe me through the cockpit doorway. His co-pilot was too busy with last minute details to look up from the controls.

"Yes, just until it's confirmed that my host is in residence." Would I be a welcome guest? Had I hurried all this way for nothing? Would the police be calling for my head for leaving the country? Would they, in the worst-case scenario, call Interpol? What did any of that matter? I just needed to find Lachlan, make things okay between us.

I scrambled to my feet and dashed down the steps leading off the plane and toward the drawbridge that was in the down position. Too impressive for words, the castle looming over the landscape had tiered towers and gaily flying banners with some pretty impressive gargoyles guarding the outer rim of the battlements.

Twilight had deepened the shadows, and whispers of *hurry, hurry* raced through my mind. I detoured around the side of the tower, running now, headed toward the back of the property. I raced across the grass. Was that Lachlan standing on the cliff? My heart squeezed hard as I prayed to the goddess to keep him safe.

"Lachlan!" I shouted at the top of my lungs, wanting him to know I'd come for him. To be with him. To give us a chance.

He turned at the sound of my voice, but his expression was impossible to read so far away. His movements faltered then, as if something beneath him had broken away. And in the worst split second of my life, he lost his footing and vanished from view.

"NO!"

My heart pounding, I sprinted the final hundred yards to where a slim margin of land had broken away. Almost unable to look over the cliff's edge, I made myself peer over, bracing myself. But instead of seeing his broken body on the rocks below or floating in the cold ocean water, Lachlan was clinging to the edge of the cliff face a few feet below.

I got down on my knees, then on my belly, reaching out for him. He swung his one arm up toward me, and I stretched out as far as I could to reach for it. When his hand clasped mine, pure electrical impulse sparked through me, giving me extra strength and courage.

"I'm too heavy for you. Let me go."

His words stunned me to the core. I shook my head. We'd either go down together, or be saved together.

Suddenly, Loki was at my side, a thick rope in his mouth. I grabbed it from him with one hand and tossed the end to Lachlan. It would serve as a last resort if our hands slipped.

Sweat dripping in my eyes, I used all my strength to slowly, inch by inch, pull Lachlan up the final distance to the top. When he was able to scramble up onto solid ground, I didn't let go. I held his hand and pulled him back from the treacherous cliff. And I still didn't let go of his hand when we were safely away. Loki stayed close to us, his big brown eyes expressing so much emotion that I understood anew how much an animal can love.

I couldn't wait another second. I had to know. "Oh, Lachlan, I'm so sorry. Can you ever forgive me?" I pressed my body against his, needing to feel his warmth, for him to feel my love for him. And most of all, needing to feel my love returned.

He hesitated, as if listening to another voice, his head cocked at a slight angle. Was I too late? Was he done with us? With me?

Please, goddess, no.

I shivered in fear and shock at what had almost happened. How could I have been so foolish? I should have known the instant attraction meant something important was going on. That everything since had confirmed it.

"I'm sorry I wasn't listening better, Lachlan, that I let my skepticism and temper get in my way."

He softened at my words and I breathed again.

"And I'm sorry for smothering you, letting my need to protect drive you away," he whispered.

"I'm here now and I want us to have that chance to begin again. Can we do that?" I asked, allowing myself to be vulnerable and open to rejection for the first time in my life. It was a huge step and I almost faltered in my resolve. *But only with taking the biggest chances can one reap the biggest rewards.* The wise words of The Creig came back to me.

"I'd like that too."

"Thank you for being you, Lachlan. For opening my life to all the amazing possibilities that it has to offer." I had never been more alive than standing on the ancient ground with my Forever Mate, a spot that had seen scores of ancients come and go. The very history of the place seeped into me, filling me up with something I didn't even know I was missing. The connection to family and place.

The sounds of a sonic jet overhead broke the stillness and we both looked upward.

"My clan has come back to Creigbourne. Time to celebrate, *mo ghràdh*."

I wanted to celebrate with Lachlan more than anything between the sheets, sensing that our reunion lovemaking would place us up among the stars, but that would have to wait. "I can't imagine anything finer than celebrating with you. I met your grandmother just before I left Vegas. A wiser woman I've never come across."

"That she is. Now kiss me before my clan runs us over with good wishes."

"Aw, music to my ears—"

Lachlan pressed his lips against mine, cutting off my words. The sensation made my body wake up and demand fulfillment. My nipples tightened and my pussy clenched around nothing in a very painful way. Did we really have to wait? Wasn't there a bush we could hide behind and enjoy each other? Now that he was safe and we'd made up, I wanted it all. No holds barred. Not that we ever had held back in the sex department, but now, knowing we were going ahead as a couple, I wanted to experience the satisfaction of making love knowing who we were and how much we meant to each other. I was damn sure it would add another whole layer of pleasure to the act.

I climbed onto Lachlan like a cat in heat, pressing myself against his amazing body with a wantonness that astonished me.

"Maybe we should be handfasted first since the family will be pouring across that field within a minute?" he murmured, his hands roaming my body in contrast to his words.

The word riveted me, helped me fight against the passion that urged we make love right then and there, filled me with realization. *Handfasted.* A permanent celebration of us. Surely love making could be held at bay a little while. Just not too long...

"I'd like that. Right here, right now. I don't want to wait, my love," I said, using the word *love* for the first time, enjoying the richness of the soft syllable flowing off my tongue and dancing through the air.

"Neither do I."

Lachlan hadn't been kidding. A stampede of clansmen was even now advancing toward us, The Creig at their head.

"Welcome to Castle Creigbourne and the Wulver Highland Heathens Clan, Esme," The Creig said when she reached us. Her white hair floated about her face from the breeze coming off the sea. The slight taste of salt stirred my senses with each breath.

"Thank you." I accepted her kiss on my cheek and gave her a wide smile in return. "You sure got here fast. Is that due to second sight?"

"Aye, lass, I visioned the two of ye saving the other. Such miracles become the stuff of legends in our world."

The others crowded round us now, giving their blessings and warm words of greeting. By the time I had met everyone, my mind was spinning.

"Come. Time to get ye ready, lass," The Creig announced.

And before I could object, I was whisked away across the field and toward the castle.

In a whirlwind of activities, I was told to have a shower, while female members of the Creig clan would see to everything. Apparently, this was considered a good day for a handfasting. The day a shifter is saved and love is proven means good luck and a life built on a sound foundation, according to The Creig.

I couldn't argue with that reasoning. Hmm, the sounds of another jet landing surprised me. Who else had arrived? The Creig began to speak again, making me forget all about it.

"This gown has been passed down from generation to generation, from matriarch to matriarch. It's now yours to wear, Esme of the House of Luceres, and to pass on to your daughters."

The long off-white dress that she held up for me to view was beyond exquisite. Handmade lace of an intricate design flowed down in panels from under the bosom. The top section was so delicately crafted it defied how anyone could have seen well enough to manage such a feat. The beautiful scalloped edging of the bodice would flatter any woman's neckline.

"It's the tree of life pattern, with each of these sections representing branches. It took years to make and it's kept protected in a humidity-controlled vault when not in use," she explained with pride.

"I'm honored but it seems almost too precious to wear." The thought of developing a tear or rent in the fine fabric horrified me.

"No fear. We can put it right if such a thing occurs. But it won't. I've seen the truth of it." The Creig's knowing expression was meant to reassure me.

I prayed she was right as I stepped into the marvel of creation and drew it up over my shoulders. When I turned around and looked in the full-length mirror I gasped aloud.

Chapter Twenty-Seven

Lachlan

My two brothers assisted me in my bedchamber to prepare for the ceremony. It seemed my fingers had become too clumsy for the job, fumbling at tying up my dress tartan and adjusting my sporran. Perhaps because my mind was racing ahead of the celebration to having Esme in my bed. I'd been fighting my need to be with her, inside her, ever since she arrived. Seeing her beautiful face, glowing with love, racing toward me across that ancient ground, it had charged me up like nothing else ever could. Though I longed to get to the passionate act of lovemaking and commitment that would lead to the final bonding, I had to stand still for this final act. I just prayed there would be no late-night shenanigans like a Chiverie where the newly handfasted couple was at the mercy of the clan who came calling, causing all sorts of grief for the pair.

"Didn't that old crone have it right, Lachlan," Calan said.

"I still say she was selkie," Logan argued.

"What old— Oh." I remembered—couldn't believe it had slipped my mind. Had it only been six months since the Spirit of Creigbourne festival? The elder prophesying with the mists of dawn rising at her back and the standing stones to her right and left was a vision not to be forgotten. She'd spoken to each of us in turn, promising a year of new beginnings and upheavals.

"You'd best both be ready for your own handfastings. Didn't she say within a year we'd all find our true mates 'in the land of desert and sage'?" I should have put two and two together sooner!

"So, all I have to do to avoid all that pain and anguish is to avoid Vegas? And I thought she said the land of desert and sin," Logan said with a smirk. He was the legendary commitment-phobic Creig. I'd like to see his reaction when he was hit by the thunderbolt, knowing he'd be as vulnerable to fate as the rest of us. He'd not be able to call his life his own until he and his new mate answered the call.

Calan remained quiet for a moment, contemplating something, judging by the look on his handsome mug. I had to admit, we three brothers cleaned up good and made our clan proud. "I had a dream the other night." Calan was our clan's enforcer, one of a select team of experts that comprised the Worldwide Security for Lycans or WSL.

"Do tell, bro," Logan said, stepping back from a final adjustment of my kilt to admire his handiwork, his head cocked to the right.

"I was lost in the desert, thirsty and hungry, bitten by every creature known to man and wolf." Calan shuddered at the memory. "Then this beautiful naked lass with masses of gorgeous white-gold hair like Lady Godiva came riding up on the back of a gleaming black stallion. What a sight! I thought for sure I was hallucinating." He paused in his recital, like he was still seeing her in real time.

"Well, did she do anything else? Or say anything?" I pressed, curious as hell. It wasn't often a wolf got to be party to such a dream. But the three of us had always been close and sharing was more common than not. Family mattered more than anything, and maybe even more so in our clan.

"Aye, but it doesn't matter."

"Afraid to say, laddie?" Logan quipped.

"Hell, no matter, she said 'twas a miracle…you know…our meeting."

"It's a damn miracle she let the likes of you see her naked!" Logan said with a wide smirk. "Did you oblige the lass in return?"

"I would have, but she took off at a gallop, doing some fancy horseback trick that looked mighty pretty atop that saddle, let me tell you!" My brother's eyes flashed neon green with the memory. Well, if the female were stark-naked, that would rile any man's wolf.

"Okay, time to get to the main event," Logan announced. "Get our brother tied to his ball and chain."

"A toast first, I'm thinking," Calan said. The pair of us ignored Logan's jab and his dismal view on marriage.

Calan grabbed a champagne magnum and poured three flutes, the bubbly liquid spilling over the tops of the glasses.

"I'm going with tradition for my blessing on the union of Lachlan and Esme. *May you both be blessed with the strength of heaven, The light of the sun and the radiance of the moon, The splendor of fire, The speed of lightning, The swiftness of wind, The depth of the sea, The stability of earth, And the firmness of rock,*" Calan said.

"All kidding aside, I wish Lachlan and his bonny lass Esme the best of all things going forward in this life together. May your wolf always run free and your lass warm your bed every night. To new beginnings."

"*To new beginnings,*" we chorused.

"Now let's get you married, bro," Logan said, clapping me on the back.

Loki, the wedding rings housed in a small velvet bag tied around his neck with a white ribbon, gave a soft chuff of agreement.

Five minutes later we stood between the standing stones that faced the open waters of the Atlantic Ocean. The ceremonial stones had been erected during the time of the Picts and had been used for any important social gathering or ceremony ever since. And today my *caileag ghrinn* and I would be handfasted within their legendary enclosure, ensuring a good, long, healthy life as Forever Mates.

The haunting sounds of the pipes began, announcing the bride's final walk as a single woman down the lace strip laid out for her on the green to where we all waited for her.

Then my Esme came into view over the rise in the land and my breath stilled in my chest. Dressed in a gown fit for a queen, a crown of gold laurel on her lovely head, she fairly danced across the remaining space between us. I knew myself to be the luckiest man and wolf in the universe to be able to spend my life with her.

Esme

I had eyes for no one but Lachlan as I made my way on winged feet toward him. The magic pull was stronger now, so obvious that I wondered how I could have missed it before. Aw, he looked so handsome standing there, dressed in his ceremonial kilt, his golden-brown hair tied back at the nape of his neck exposing his chiseled features.

To spend my life with him, to pledge my love before kith and kin, because yes, my family had flown in on the third jet for the proceedings. Only Meghan couldn't make it due to work commitments, much to her sorrow. And with the welcome news that the real murderer had been arrested after my pack had worked with Lachlan's to expose the culprit, life was perfect.

Tears welled in my eyes at thought of my mother not being able to see this day. I blinked them away, sensing her presence looking down on me, blessing me.

I glanced over at the two brothers, Calan and Logan, so proud of their brother and so fierce in their kilts, sensing they too had a heart connection to Vegas.

My heart filling with almost more love than I could bear, I stepped up to the standing stones to pledge my life to the best man — and wolf — in the entire universe for me.

Want to see more from this author? Here's a taster for you to enjoy!

Sin City Kilts: Soul of Iron
January Bain

Excerpt

Calan

The night wind lashed the casement windows of Castle Creigbourne, driving rain against the tower's glass. The din woke me from a battle I was winning, striking down the enemy with my mighty claymore that I'd named Slayer. *They don't accuse me of having an iron soul for nothing. I never give up, and danger's my life's blood, even in my dreams.*

Stretching, then grimacing as the numerous cuts and bruises from my recent cage fight made themselves known, I checked the time. Five a.m. *Early enough to avoid company.* I treasured time alone, a rare commodity in the Creig clan.

My bleary vision was made worse by a pounding headache curtesy of a night spent in our local pub celebrating the Burryman and my earlier knockout victory of a worthy opponent. I rubbed my eyes, blinked and spied my cell phone lying by the bed, reminding me of the encrypted email I'd gotten last night.

Right. Today my attendance was requested at virtual council. More like demanded, but also to be expected as my clan's enforcer and one of a select team of experts that composed the Worldwide Security for Lycans or WSL. The position was made for me...when I didn't have a damn hangover. Well, a good run across the moors would clear my head of the remaining cobwebs.

With no thought to dress, I strode naked from the room and took the stairs leading to the outdoors two at a time, exiting from the back of the keep. The scent of heather and moss stirred my senses as the rain ceased and a rainbow appeared over a rise in the land. I transformed to my other nature, entering through the glimmering doorway in the dimension next door, then exiting the portal as wolf. That split-second moment in time when my energy shifted, then reformed, exposing my wild nature, never got old.

On my massive paws, I loped across the wet green fields of Eilean maddah-allaidh or Wolf Island, eager to patrol our vast holdings and check for any interloper or breach of security. No one who knew of our piece of off-the-beaten-path real estate took the chance of riling one of us, the Highland Heathen Clan born of Wulvers and Vikings and ancient warriors, but I still kept a sharp lookout for the unexpected.

Someone finding our shores and causing havoc could not, and would not, be tolerated. The freedom of our heritage needed to continue, and I would protect my clan and our secrets to my dying breath. It explained why I'd chosen to live my life on my own, not willing to allow another to suffer if it was cut short. Not that I intended that to happen, but in this world, shit happened.

I was halfway across the island when my nose picked up a scent. I skirted the area, recognizing the perfume of a woman best left to her own devices. Last thing I needed was giving Sherry, a cousin with whom I'd shared a mutual love of fine whiskey in the pub last night, any hope of us spending time together, old friend or not.

The longer route took me past Wulver Cave, and I slipped inside to quench my thirst. I had a secure location that no one, not even my clan, was aware of in the Highlands. I keep it fully stocked and ready in case of a need to evacuate my entire family at a moment's notice. Thankfully to date, there had been no need for its use.

At the edge of the underground freshwater lake, a feature of Wulver Cave, I peered around, making sure I was alone and not about to be ambushed by one of my brothers or cousins. It would be just like them to sneak up on me and try to pin me down. *As if.* It would just lead to a fight, then a standoff, something my headache could do without, though the fresh air was helping it fade.

I bent to lap the water with my tongue, then stilled as a vision appeared on its mirrorlike surface. *Danger.* An unknown wolf. Strange stripes marred its back. I swung my massive head around but there was no presence behind me or anywhere in the cave. *It was a warning then.* But where was this wolf? This interloper? Lachlan was the one of us blessed with second sight. This was normally his domain, being first born. Why was I being shown the image? Perhaps being enforcer, it was sent to me to aid in protecting my clan?

Grateful for the advance warning but growling with deadly intent over there being a threat somewhere that needed answering, I left the cave. I needed to speak with my brothers, warn them.

In the shadow of Castle Creigbourne, I shifted back to human and strode inside, prepared to shower and dress before tracking down Lachlan and Logan, and ten minutes later I entered the huge kitchen, spotting my quarry breaking their fast.

"Morning," Lachlan said, the intensity of his glance his normal modus operandum.

Logan was too busy stuffing his face to bother looking my way. The baby of our family, he was all about fulfilling his own physical needs first. *Spoiled doesn't cover it.* I might have been left to my own devices the most, being the middle child, but I was glad of it. I had a duty and commitment to my clan that few, if any, could match. My brother was studying film for heaven's sake, hardly the kind of pursuit our ancestors would have agreed with.

"Out patrolling again?" Lachlan asked.

Logan shook his head. "You know you don't have to do that, right? Waste of time in my opinion. No one in their right mind would attack us here."

"And what if they're not in their right mind?" I answered. "You just going to pretend psychopaths and usurpers don't exist?"

"Better than thinking something's hiding behind every rock, bro."

"You got something to say, spit it out, Logan."

"I think you've said enough, Logan," Lachlan, the clan's alpha admonished him. "What's up, Calan? You seem even more paranoid than usual. Something going on?"

I sat down across the expansive table from the pair and dove into the pancakes, sausages and eggs, a morning favorite. "Yeah, something's going on all right," I said after swallowing a bite of the food I'd piled my plate with.

"Something do with that lass I saw you drinking with last night?" Logan asked, slipping in a zinger from another angle. Incorrigible summed him up. I pitied the female that tried to straighten him out. Or maybe I pitied him more, for what female would put up with him? I did envy Lachlan and his female Esme. A perfect pairing and one that would keep them happy and blessed for their whole lives.

"I love them and leave them, bro. No other way for it," I answered.

"Me too. I just prefer to acknowledge that one might be my Forever Mate," Logan said. "Maybe I'll get lucky like Lachlan."

"Not bloody likely. No she-wolf would put up with the likes of you. She'd need a lobotomy first," I said, enjoying the instant look of anger that replaced Logan's customary smugness.

"Better than needing a heart or soul, Iron Man." Logan pretended my hit hadn't landed.

Or maybe it didn't—he was so full of it. Well, confidence cannot be underrated, though true bravery in battle was of far more vital importance than interactions with the opposite sex, in my opinion.

My Iron Man tag, which our clan tied to the warrior god, Lugh, of Celtic fame, beat Logan's Aengus, male god of love and youth, all to hell. Though on second thoughts, as someone had to continue our bloodlines, it had best be someone not heading into danger at every opportunity. An image of my best friend Galen rose, reminding me of the downside of being an enforcer and making my heart squeeze for the devastating loss to his family.

"Let's finish up. We've got that council meeting in five minutes." Lachlan glanced at the clock.

His words woke me from thoughts I would prefer to avoid and normally managed to keep squashed down flat in the back of my mind.

We got up and made our way to the library where all virtual meetings took place, in front of the big screen. Lachlan fired up the equipment and locked onto the weblink.

"Good tidings from the Highland Heathen Clan to the Houses of Luceres, Anche and Ribelle," Lachlan said as the three alphas came on stream.

Polite interactions out of the way, Cristaldo, of the House of Luceres, the most powerful and rich family of werewolves in America, spoke first, as was his right.

"There's been a disturbing incident in the desert just outside Vegas. Someone got sloppy and was caught on video shifting of all things! I don't have to tell any of you of what vital importance this is to security. In the interests of all Lycans, we need to squash this video. Now. We've never been exposed like this before. No one knows how we really shift, only gathering their intel from books and movies. This shift was the real deal."

My heartrate jacked up. This was bad news. I wanted to throttle the culprit. "Any leads on who made the recording?" I jumped in. *So, the vision in the cave holds merit.*

"A person with the online tag of Miracle. Don't even know if they're male or female. So far, the video's only been posted on the dark web. But this needs addressing now."

"I'm leaving now," I said. "Expect me ASAP."

No one disagreed with me, of course. This was my express domain.

"I'll have someone meet you when you arrive, Calan," Cristaldo said.

"Have the other members of WSL been alerted?" I asked. If not, I'd call them in as needed.

"No, we called you first."

After the meeting concluded and the video feed had been turned off, Lachlan turned to me, suspicion clear in his green eyes. "You knew something of this?"

"I was going to tell you I saw something in Wulver Cave before His Highness interrupted." I jerked my head in the screen's direction. "A strange wolf with unusual stripping on its back." I shrugged. "That was it, nothing else."

"I know you can be trusted to get to the bottom of it, Calan. Go with my blessing."

"Mine too, bro," Logan said. And for once he did look sincere. Well, when push came to shove, we did stick together.

No one had better badmouth one of our clan, if they knew what was good for them.

About the Author

January Bain has wished on every falling star, every blown-out birthday candle and every coin thrown in a fountain to be a storyteller. To share the tales of high adventure, mysteries and full-blown thrillers she has dreamed of all her life. The story you now have in your hands is the compilation of a lot of things manifesting itself for this special series.

If you are looking for January Bain, you can find her hard at work every morning without fail in her office with two furry babies trying to prove who does a better job of guarding the doorway. And, of course, she's married to the most romantic man! Who once famously replied to her protest about buying fresh flowers for their home every week with, "Give me one good reason why not?" Leaving her speechless and knocking her head against the proverbial wall for being so darn foolish. She loves flowers.

If you wish to connect in the virtual world, she is easily found on Facebook, Twitter and writes a weekly blog about her journey on Blogger. Oh, and she loves to talk books…

January loves to hear from readers. You can find her contact information, website details and author profile page at https://www.totallybound.com

Home of Erotic Romance

Sign up for our newsletter and find out about all our
romance book releases, eBook sales and promotions,
sneak peeks and FREE romance books!